The arm that sn
waist lifted her

As she was crushed against a chest that felt as solid as oak, her gun was stripped from her hand. She kicked back with her right foot, the heel of her boot making satisfying contact with the shin of whoever held her. At the same time, she twisted, trying to free herself.

"Stop it," the man who'd captured her growled against her ear. "It's me. Underwood."

Intent on her struggles, it took a second for that identification to sink in.

Before it did, as if to emphasize his command, he shook her, hard enough to make her teeth snap together. "Stop it or you're going to get us both killed."

His breath was warm on her cheek. The stubble she'd noticed the night he'd come to the station moved against her skin. As unreasonable as it seemed, given the situation, she felt that same rush of sexual awareness she'd experienced this afternoon.

"Okay," she whispered. "Okay."

GAYLE WILSON

FLASHBACK

TORONTO NEW YORK LONDON
AMSTERDAM PARIS SYDNEY HAMBURG
STOCKHOLM ATHENS TOKYO MILAN MADRID
PRAGUE WARSAW BUDAPEST AUCKLAND

To Denise, with much gratitude for the opportunity
to write another Intrigue

Recycling programs
for this product may
not exist in your area.

ISBN-13: 978-0-373-69562-1

FLASHBACK

Copyright © 2011 by Mona Gay Thomas

www.Harlequin.com

Printed in U.S.A.

ABOUT THE AUTHOR

Gayle Wilson is a two-time RITA® Award winner, taking home the RITA® Award for Best Romantic Suspense Novel in 2000 and for Best Romantic Novella in 2004. In addition to twice winning the prestigious RITA® Award, Gayle's books have garnered more than 50 other awards and nominations.

Gayle was on the board of directors of Romance Writers of America for four years. In 2006 she served as the president of RWA, the largest genre-writers' organization in the world. She has written for Harlequin Historicals, Harlequin Intrigue, Special Releases, HQN Books, MIRA, and Mills & Boon.

Please visit her website at www.BooksByGayleWilson.com.

Books by Gayle Wilson

CAST OF CHARACTERS

Eden Reddick—The unsolved disappearance of her sister shattered Eden Reddick's childhood. When a little girl is kidnapped in a manner that eerily echoes that long-ago mystery, Eden, now the chief of police of Waverly, Mississippi, has an opportunity to prevent that same tragedy from destroying the lives of another family.

Jake Underwood—The ex-special forces major paid a heavy price for his service to his country, a sacrifice Jake thought he'd made peace with—until a terrified child inexplicably shows up in one of his flashbacks.

Raine Nolan—Raine is taken from her own bed and from the same room in which her sister is sleeping—exactly as Eden's sister was kidnapped more than two decades before and in a place hundreds of miles from this small Southern town.

Margo Nolan—Raine's mother has no choice but to cling to the belief that Eden has the skill and determination to find her daughter—because the alternative is simply unthinkable.

Ray Nolan—Raine's father is the prime suspect in his daughter's disappearance. Is Eden's faith in his innocence colored by her love for her own father?

Dean Partlow—Eden's deputy chief, who has been not only her mentor, but also her friend, brings his expertise in police work as well as his knowledge of the area to the investigation, but will it be enough to find the missing child in time?

Dr. Benjamin Murphy—Nobody knows Waverly and its people better than Doc Murphy, but it is questions about Jake Underwood that bring Eden to his door.

Prologue

The aura was like how people describe a migraine. Except it wasn't. There was no pain. And nothing he could take to prevent what he knew was about to happen.

He leaned against the side of his truck, waiting for the inevitable—that burst of light or energy or whatever it was that marked the disappearance of the present and the return of the sights and sounds and smells of the day his life had changed forever.

What he smelled mostly was the diesel fuel. Smoke. And the blood, of course, but that came later.

What he heard—immediately and until the very end—were the screams. Those echoed and reechoed in his nightmares as well, but never with the intensity they had in the flashbacks.

This time the force of the transition was so strong it battered him physically. Although he wasn't conscious of the movement, his knees buckled, throwing him to the ground beside the pickup.

Bile rose in his throat as he waited for the rest. Carter's shrieked profanities, intermingled with pleas to the Virgin, as he tried to stuff his intestines back inside his body. The sound of the second RPG striking the vehicle behind them.

After that came the smells. All of them. Everything that signified agony and death and loss.

This time, however, there was an almost eerie stillness. He

opened his eyes—although he'd never been able to ascertain if they really closed during these episodes—and found not the monochromatic sameness of the desert landscape that had always been there before, but a pit. A hole. Something dark and sinister, although he couldn't identify anything else about it.

And instead of Carter's screams, all he heard was water dripping. The slow, steady pulse of a leak or of condensation off the overwhelming dampness that now surrounded him. He shivered against its chill, fighting a primordial response to its blackness.

He had no idea where he was. Or why he was here. All he knew was that he was terrified, a gut-level fear his extensive combat experience didn't alleviate.

He wanted to close his eyes again. To hide from the cold, terrifying darkness. To deny its existence.

As his lids began to fall, he caught a peripheral glimpse of something else that shouldn't be here. Not in this cave, this hole, this wherever it was.

Not in his flashback.

Before he could fully open his eyes again, it was all gone. He was suddenly back in the present, kneeling in the dirt beside his truck, his mouth dry as old bones, his hands trembling.

He knew from experience that the episode had lasted only seconds. Despite its short duration, his entire body was drenched with sweat. His chest heaved as he tried to slow his racing heart before it exploded.

After a moment, he leaned his forehead against the comforting heat of the metal beside him. His pulse finally nearing something approaching normal, he stifled the sobs that tore at his chest.

Always the same reaction. An urge to shed the tears he hadn't shed then. Or consciously since.

He denied them now, finally lifting his gaze to the branches of the massive oak that stretched above his head. Concentrating on controlling his breathing, he watched the Spanish moss draped over them sway in the breeze off the Gulf.

Something about its motion helped ground him in reality. In the present.

That's why he'd come back. Back to what had once been home. Although there was no one here now who constituted family, this place was as close to the feeling of safety that word connoted as he had ever found.

He looked around, relieved that since he'd been back, this had only happened here. The house was isolated enough that it was unlikely anyone would ever witness an episode. He wanted to keep it that way.

He licked his lips and then began the struggle to rise to his feet. Despite the months of therapy the Army had provided, there were still lingering physical effects from his injuries.

He had finally reconciled himself to the reality that there always would be. He was lucky to be alive. Luckier than Carter. Or Martinez. Chan. Luckier than he deserved.

He wasn't going to whine about what he'd lost. Not even about the occasional reimmersion into the past. Into that particular day.

Except it hadn't *been* that day, he remembered, as he grasped the door handle to pull himself up. Not this time. This time…

He closed his eyes, trying to bring the images from the flashback, or whatever it had been, into his consciousness again, but there was nothing there. Nothing but an aching sense of cold. And darkness. And an unspeakable horror.

Uncomfortable with the return of those sensations, he began to open his eyes. As he did, he remembered the other thing that had been in that place. The last image he had seen—half seen—before he'd been brutally catapulted into the present.

He didn't understand why she was there, but there was no

doubt in his mind she had been. A little girl with blond hair. Maybe four or five. Maybe older. His knowledge of children was limited enough that he couldn't be sure.

He was certain only that she'd been there with him. In that pit. That black hole.

And that, like him, she, too, had been absolutely terrified.

Chapter One

"Can you tell me about it, Mrs. Nolan? The moment you found out your daughter was missing?" Eden Reddick leaned forward, establishing eye contact—and hopefully, a feeling of trust—with the woman on the opposite couch.

Totally focused on the story she was about to hear, Eden blocked out the other aspects of the investigation going on around them. Her deputy chief, Dean Partlow, was taking the father outside to hear his version of events, as she was preparing to guide the mother through hers. The officers she'd assigned to gather evidence from the bedrooms upstairs had already disappeared, leaving the two of them alone in the spotless living room.

Margo Nolan nodded in response to Eden's prodding. Her tear-reddened eyes shifted slightly off center, as if she were seeing it all again.

"I went to wake the kids up for school. It's really preschool for the twins, but with the older ones and all, we just call everything school. I usually wake the girls first because they're the easiest to get going. I lay out their clothes, and then, while they dress, I wake Gavin and Casey. This morning I went into their room and Raine wasn't there. Storm was asleep, but her sister—" The sentence broke, and Eden patiently waited through the pause. "I thought maybe she was in the bathroom, you know, but she wasn't. And she wasn't in the hall or in the boys' room. By that time, I was yellin' at the top of my lungs. Just pure screamin' for her to answer me." Her eyes found Eden's again. "I was already startin' to get scared, but tellin' myself that was stupid. What in the world could happen to her inside her own house?"

In her own bed...

Eden's mother had used that phrase over and over. "She was in her own bed. Where would you think a child could be safer than in her own bed?"

"But she wasn't anywhere," Margo went on. "By then, everybody was looking. Ray and the boys. Me. Looking inside and out. We kept askin' Storm, but she just kept sayin' she didn't know. All she knew was that Raine had been there when she went to sleep."

"How long before you called 911?"

Margo shook her head. "I don't know. Maybe an hour. Maybe more. You just keep thinkin' she's gonna be *somewhere*. You sure don't want to think about someone takin' your baby. Not here. Not in Waverly."

The nearest town to this tiny Mississippi community was the coastal resort of Pascagoula. And few people *there* would think about the possibilities of someone kidnapping a child from her own bedroom.

Margo shook her head again, dabbing at her eyes with a tissue from the box that sat on the coffee table between them. "Then the officers found the door to the patio had been forced. That's when I knew—" She stopped, bowing her head as she held the tissue bunched against her nose and mouth.

"We've already got people out looking for her," Eden said, as comfort. "And we're working on the Amber Alert. That's when people begin thinking about what they've seen and reporting things that seemed...strange. Out of place."

Margo looked up at that, nodding vigorously. "That's what Ray keeps sayin'. It just takes the right lead. We just need that one person to come forward."

The father's language, almost official, struck a warning note in Eden's mind, but she kept any sign of that unease from the mother, choosing to reassure her instead. "I'm sure we'll hear something soon. I can arrange for you to make a public plea for people to do that, if you'd like."

The parents' statement had become the standard operating procedure in these situations. And the local stations would be more than willing to give it airtime.

While Eden knew that if the Nolans chose to speak publicly, generating sympathy for theirs and their daughter's plight, it might increase the odds of a witness coming forward, she also dreaded the onslaught of national attention that might generate. It would be a mixed blessing, in her opinion, getting Raine Nolan's description out to a far larger audience than the local affiliates could, but at the same time bringing more of the outside media into this mostly rural area.

"They find missin' children all the time." Margo seemed stuck on reiterating the assurances she'd been given. "Raine will get home safe, too. I just know it."

Eden nodded, torn between pity and guilt that she couldn't be nearly that sanguine about the outcome. She stood, indicating the front door with a sideways tilt of her head. "I'll go on outside and tell the TV people you want to speak to the public on your daughter's behalf. You think your husband will want to say something?"

"I don't know that Ray will get up in front of the camera. I've always been the outgoin' one in the family. Me and the girls." Her eyes flicked to the pictures of her twin daughters in the photos lining the hallway. "The boys are into sports. Ray says that breeds the kind of physical confidence they need. All I know is they don't have the kind that lets you get up in front of a crowd. The kind that lets you speak up for yourself. That's what my girls have. Raine's probably tellin' whoever's taken her to get her on back home or she's gonna be late for school." Margo's laugh was watery. "I can just hear her now."

Eden's personal acquaintance with the reality of what the Nolans faced left her unable to respond to that sad attempt at humor with another platitude. "Right now, we just need to get the information out to the public," she said instead. "Television and the Alert are the best ways to do that."

"I'd really appreciate you settin' all that up," Margo said. "I swear, everybody's been so good. Ray said the neighbors have already organized search parties. With all this help, I know we'll find her soon. We're just bound to."

Eden nodded again, and this time made good her escape through the front door. Given the possibility that Raine Nolan had been kidnapped as early as midnight, they were already eight hours into this.

She knew, even if Margo Nolan didn't yet seem to understand, that whoever had snatched that little girl out of her own bed could be several hundred miles away by now. In any direction. Even, she acknowledged with a chill of resignation, out into the Gulf.

TAKING HER DEPUTY chief with her, Eden had retreated to the squad car to avoid the mob of local media already assembling along the street in front of the Nolans' house. Although their presence was inevitable, and ultimately useful, at this stage of the investigation she felt only resentment that keeping them out of the yard and away from potential evidence required three of her officers, who could have been better employed in the search.

"The local affiliates will want to broadcast it, too, of course," Dean Partlow said, "but the cable-news guys can give us a wider audience."

"God knows we need one," Eden agreed.

Dean had been a friend of her father's. To give him credit, no matter what he thought about having a woman, and a much younger woman at that, as his chief, he had never indicated by word or deed that he didn't believe Eden was capable of doing the job she had virtually inherited.

The town they served was small, the kind where everyone knew everybody else's business. Eden was sure the older man knew more about hers than she would be comfortable with, but that was something else Dean hadn't let on about. Just as he'd never indicated that he felt he was more deserving of the job her dad had groomed her for most of her life.

She was grateful Partlow had stayed on when her father retired. She'd learned almost as much from Dean in the past three years as she had from her dad or the criminal-justice courses she'd taken.

Part of that acquired knowledge was how unprepared she'd been to accept the responsibility that had been handed to her. Something that had only made her more determined to eventually become worthy of it.

"I don't know about that," Dean said. "I can't think of a single case where a parent's tearful plea has made a hill of beans worth of difference in the outcome."

"You got an opinion about who did this? Other than you don't think the mother was involved?"

"I don't get paid to have opinions. Not at this stage. 'Course, so far, we ain't got much fact to go on, either."

Almost all they knew right now was that Raine Nolan was missing. Like Dean, Eden found it hard to believe Margo was involved. Her grief and innocent hopefulness had felt too genuine.

"What'd you think about the father?" she asked.

"If Ray Nolan's faking, he should be making movies instead of selling insurance. I've seen men with that kind of burden of guilt on 'em, and that *isn't* what's in his eyes this morning."

"What is?" Eden needed him to put it into words, maybe just to reinforce what her own instincts were telling her.

"Disbelief. Fear. Fury. Somebody stole his baby. Somebody who didn't have any right to be inside his house, much less take a child out of it."

"You know that the parents' involvement is the first thing the FBI is going to suggest, especially in a case like this. Somebody comes in and snatches a little girl out of the same room where her sister's sleeping."

"Just because that's the most common scenario doesn't make it the explanation for this."

"So who do you think took her? And why? They're going to ask, and right now..." Eden shook her head.

"Nobody's asked for ransom. Not yet, anyways. And despite that big ole house, Ray hasn't got much money. None he could get to real quick. The other possibilities are a whole lot less appealing."

"You think she's dead," Eden said flatly.

"I think there's a real good chance. My worse fear is the kid'll be alive and we'll walk right by her. Or we don't search the house she's in. Do something stupid when, if we'd been quicker or smarter, we could have found her."

That was something Eden didn't want to think about. The fact that a little girl's life rested in her hands. That if she forgot something, missed the obvious or was just unlucky, Raine Nolan might die.

"We'll need to have them add a plea that anyone who's noticed anything unusual, anything at all, should call the hotline," she said.

People in the South were sometimes hesitant to report what their neighbors were doing, even if they thought it was strange. They could only hope sympathy for the mother's desperation would overcome the public's tendency to mind their own business.

"Have 'em keep that number up while Margo talks," Dean suggested.

Eden nodded, adding to her notes. "Maybe you're wrong,

Dean. Maybe somebody looked at the Nolans from the outside and thought they have money."

"I hope so. For all our sakes."

Eden glanced up, meeting his eyes. "You don't think anybody's going to call."

Dean hesitated before he shook his head. "That same instinct that's telling me Ray and Margo don't have anything to do with this is telling me that whoever forced open their patio door and took that baby didn't do it for money."

Chapter Two

"Can you think of anything we haven't done?"

Eden's question was as much to herself as to Dean. As hard as it was to believe, they were now approaching the infamous forty-eight-hour mark on Raine Nolan's kidnapping. And despite doing everything she could think of, they were no closer to finding her than they had been when the call had come in yesterday morning.

"Pray?" Dean looked up as he took a bite out of one of the sandwiches someone had brought into Eden's office hours ago.

The take-out iced teas that had accompanied them had formed puddles of condensation on the glass cover of her desk. The possibility of food poisoning crossed her mind, but it wasn't enough to keep her from biting into her own sandwich.

"I expect folks who are more adept at praying than either of us have that covered. What'd the lab tell you?"

"That they're six months behind, but that since it concerns a child, they'll do the best they can."

Chronically underfunded, the state forensics lab was their only option. The county didn't handle enough crime to justify having one of their own.

Not that the guys who had gathered the evidence had been all that optimistic that there was anything in the girls' room that would point a finger in the perpetrator's direction. The best they could hope for was something that might be useful at the trial.

If there ever *was* a trial…

"The Bureau's questioning the Nolans again." Dean shrugged as he added the information.

"You think they got their minds made up?"

"Looks that way. I'm not sure it matters, though. Long as you don't."

It would be easier, God knows, to think that whatever had happened to Raine was over and done. An out-of-control moment by an exhausted parent that ended in tragedy.

That image, disturbing as it was, was more palatable than those that had played in Eden's head the past two days. The only way she'd found to defeat them was to keep herself mentally occupied by making sure the department was covering every possible angle.

"They say a camera doesn't lie," she said. "I don't see how anybody who watched Margo yesterday morning could doubt she doesn't have a clue what happened to her daughter."

"So…you like Ray for this?"

"I didn't say that. You don't, and I trust your instincts. I just haven't watched him get emotional like I've watched Margo."

That was one thing she'd have to give the national media credit for. They'd given the mother's plea to bring her daughter home endless airtime. The fact that they'd apparently had a couple of slow news days had played into that, of course, but the story itself was compelling enough to demand attention.

Where would you think a child would be safer than in her own bed?

Banishing the memory of her mother's voice, Eden took another bite of her sandwich. The silence that fell as they ate was companionable. And she had leaned heavily on Dean's experience and his knowledge of the region and its people through these endless hours.

"Anything new from the hotline?"

Dean laughed. "Last I heard, a boatload of garbage. That's better than nothing, I guess. Better than folks not calling. You just got to weed through it all to find something that might be helpful."

"And have they found that?"

"Not that I heard."

Eden let it drop, concentrating on finishing her supper. More an act of refueling than anything else. After the long hours between this and breakfast, she'd needed it.

The knock on the glass top half of her office door disturbed the silence. She motioned with one hand, giving Winton Grimes permission to enter. As it had half a dozen times today, her heart began to race a bit in anticipation of what he might have come to tell them.

"Got something?" she asked as he opened the door and stuck his head in.

"You said you wanted to hear anything we thought might be...significant."

"Yeah?"

"Well, okay, this is a little bit... Hell," Winton said with an embarrassed grin, "it's a whole *lot* off the beaten path, but I thought since we ain't got much of nothing else, you all might want to hear it."

"So tell us." Dean's tone suggested he'd listened to enough hemming and hawing.

"If this wasn't who it is, I might have just let it go, but..."

"Damn it, Winton," Dean exploded, "spit it out. Nobody's got time for your pussyfooting. Not today."

"It's okay, Winton," Eden soothed. "We want to hear. Whatever it is."

"Jake Underwood."

Eden couldn't quite identify the sound Dean made in

response to the name. Laughter? An expression of disbelief? Whatever it had been, Winton stopped again, his thin lips flattening.

"Who's Jake Underwood?"

Her question brought the young deputy's eyes back to her, but it was Dean who answered.

"His grandmother was Miz Etta Wells. The Wells that was one of the founding families. Jake spent summers here when he was a kid."

Eden waited, but neither man seemed inclined to go on. Finally she prodded, "And you've got some reason to believe he may have had something to do with the Nolan girl's disappearance."

"It's not that," Winton said. "At least…not exactly."

The sound Dean made this time was clearly one of contempt. Eden couldn't be sure, however, whether that had been directed at Jake Underwood or the deputy.

"Then *exactly* what is it?" She tried to imbue her voice with the same authority her father's seemed to command naturally. Apparently, it was effective.

With another glance at the older man, Grimes began to talk. "Underwood says she's in a cave or something underground. Says somebody's keeping her down there. He says it's wet and dark, and all you can hear is water dripping."

There was a long silence. Since she'd asked the question, Eden felt it was up to her to break it. "Is that it?"

"Yeah. Except he said she's scared. *Terrified* is the word he used."

Despite the fact that she had no basis for believing the validity of any of that description, it had chilled Eden. A four-year-old child kept in the dark *would* be terrified. Anyone would know that. How Mr. Underwood could know the Nolan child was there was another question.

"And he knows all this *how?*"

There was another hesitation, and another glance at Dean, before Grimes answered. "Says he saw it in a flashback."

Flashback. The term produced images of 9/11. Or of soldiers from her father's generation who'd come back damaged mentally from a jungle hell. How the word could possibly apply to a child who'd been kidnapped this morning...

"*Flashback?* You sure that's what he said?"

"Yes, ma'am. Look, I told you this is out there. And if it was anybody but him, I wouldn't have told you."

"You *believe* him?" Dean's tone expressed the same contempt as his earlier snort.

The kid stood his ground. "Like I said, if this was anybody else..."

"You keep saying that," Eden tried to clarify. "What does it mean?"

"It means he thinks Underwood's a hero," Dean answered, "and therefore exempt from the same commonsense scrutiny he'd give anybody else coming in here with that cock-and-bull story."

"That's not—"

Dean didn't allow the deputy to finish. "God knows, I don't want to speak ill of somebody who's served their country. But the truth is Jake came back from his last tour a little less put together than when he left."

"From his last tour" and "who's served his country" were obviously references to the military. What Eden didn't understand was the cryptic finish. "'Less put together'?"

"Head injury. Along with some other stuff. It's the brain damage, though, that would put thoughts of seeing that little girl into Jake's head. And that's all this is, you hear me." The last was clearly directed at Grimes. "You go spouting this story around town, and you're liable to get somebody hurt. Somebody who sure as hell doesn't deserve to be hurt."

"Then...you don't think this man might have had something to do with the kidnapping?" Eden asked. "I mean, someone who's brain-damaged *and* having visions of a missing child… Seems to me that makes him a *prime* candidate."

It didn't make sense for Dean to dismiss the idea out of hand, although she couldn't argue with the warning he'd just issued. If the people of this town thought one of their own had been involved in Raine's kidnapping, emotions would definitely run high. That was something the department, its resources stretched to the limits, shouldn't have to deal with.

"You talk to him, Chief," Grimes said. "See what you think. That's all I'm asking."

"Oh, trust me," Eden assured him, getting up, "I'm going to talk to him. Just forgive me if I'm a little less receptive to his story than you seem to be."

Her heart was actually pounding, blood rushing through her veins like thunder. Since the call had come in about the kidnapping, this seemed to be the first potentially important piece of the puzzle they were trying to solve.

Of course, it was always possible the brain damage Dean referred to had caused this guy to hallucinate about the crime, given the second-by-second media coverage that had been going on all day. But it was equally possible, she decided, that a man deranged by the horrors of war and by injury had seen an attractive child around town—

Eden broke the thought, determined not to speculate about this guy's motives, or his guilt or innocence, until she had more information. "Where is he?"

"I put him in the conference room. I thought that might offer more privacy."

"For him or the department?" Eden asked, as she made her way across the office.

Winton didn't answer. She was aware that the two men trailed her as she walked down the hall to the room they used for department meetings.

Operating under the influence of the adrenaline flooding her system, Eden opened the door and then realized she hadn't even stopped to think about the best way to question someone who might be classified as a prime suspect.

The man who'd been seated at the long conference table stood up, his back suddenly ramrod straight. And for his next trick, Eden thought cynically, he'll snap off a salute.

"Mr. Underwood?"

"Yes, ma'am."

His posture was the only thing remotely military about the man standing before her. Dark stubble covered his lean cheeks. His hair, blue-black under the fluorescents, was badly in need of a trim.

She also noted, her survey automatic, that his clothing, although nondescript, appeared to be clean. The threadbare jeans, white T-shirt and boots were practically de riguer for a certain type of Southern male, though she'd met enough bright, hardworking "good old boys" not to characterize anyone strictly by his dress.

Still, she acknowledged as she walked across to the table, her reaction was not the same as it would have been had Underwood been wearing a suit. Or a uniform.

"I understand you told Deputy Grimes that you've seen the Nolan girl."

The steel-gray eyes shifted to the doorway. Eden didn't turn, understanding that the ex-soldier was silently chastising Grimes for not making the situation clear. Neither she nor the deputy bothered to disabuse him of that notion.

"If he told you that, ma'am, he was mistaken. I haven't *seen* her. Not physically."

"Then how?" The question sounded confrontational, which wasn't the tack she should be taking.

The thought that this man might have harmed a little girl infuriated her. Even if Dean was right, and he hadn't been responsible, the idea that he could be in any way, shape or form pulling their chain about this—

"I have flashbacks. Yesterday morning..." The soft words

halted as Underwood took a breath, one deep enough to move the strongly defined pectoral muscles underneath the thin T-shirt. "A child—a little girl—was in the one that morning."

"In a flashback about Iraq?"

"This one wasn't. I don't know where it was. I was in a place that was wet and dark and cold. Then, just before it all disappeared...there was a child in there, too."

"Raine Nolan," Eden suggested flatly.

"I don't know. The image lasted only a second. It was... almost an impression, rather than an actual sighting. I told him that." Underwood indicated the young deputy with a lift of his chin. "But after I heard about the kidnapping, I wondered if maybe..."

"Maybe what?" Dean's question brought the ex-soldier's head up.

"If maybe I was somehow connected to her."

"And how would that happen? That 'connection,' I mean." *You son of a bitch,* Eden thought as she asked her question. *If you did something to that little girl...*

"I don't know. It just... The longer this went on, the more I wondered if somehow, in her terror..."

"You told Deputy Grimes she was terrified. If you didn't even get a good look at her, how could you tell what she was feeling?"

Underwood took another breath, his lips tightening briefly before he spoke. "Because I was feeling it, too."

"Terrified?"

She was blowing this, Eden realized, her skepticism too obvious. A good interrogator would be more sympathetic. Less hostile. She knew that, but she couldn't get the images of what a man this size and this muscular could do to a four-year-old out of her head.

"Look, I don't blame you for not believing me. I just thought I needed to let someone know. Just in case, as insane as it sounds, that there might be some connection between what I saw and the Nolan girl."

There might be some connection, all right. But not the one you're trying to sell.

"Why don't you sit down, Mr. Underwood, and tell us everything."

"That *is* everything. I realize you think I'm crazy. Believe me, you aren't the first." There was a bitter amusement underlying the comment. "In this case, you're probably right. As I said, I just thought, if there was the remotest possibility something helpful might come of what I saw…" He hesitated, clearly waiting for their response. When no one said anything, he turned and took a step, obviously heading for the door.

"Where were you Tuesday night?"

It took a second before he reacted, but whatever damage Jake Underwood's brain had suffered didn't keep him from figuring out where she was going.

"I was home. In bed. Asleep. And whatever you're thinking, you can think again. I didn't have anything to do with that child's disappearance. I came here because I was trying to help."

"By telling us you 'saw' her in a flashback."

"Obviously, it wasn't a flashback. I don't know what it was. All I know is what I saw."

"I thought it was just an impression."

"That's right. An impression that I was in a dark, wet place with a terrified little girl."

Until now, despite the absurdity of his claim, Underwood's tone had been reasonable. As if he were trying to explain things to someone whose IQ didn't quite come up to his standards. This time, however, there was a definite hint of anger in his response.

And Eden intended to use it to her advantage. "Anybody there with her? Her abductor, maybe?"

"There was nobody else."

"Well, you see, that's what makes me wonder."

"Whatever you're *wondering,* you can forget. I told you. I didn't have anything to do with her disappearance."

"She just somehow…showed up in your flashback."

"Yes." The single syllable was cold, controlled, but patently furious.

"What do you think was the reason for that, Mr. Underwood?"

"I have no idea, Chief Reddick." His sarcasm echoed hers.

"I think you do."

"I don't give a damn what you think. I came here because I thought it was my duty to tell law enforcement what I'd seen. What you do with the information is now up to you."

He rounded the table and walked toward the door. Eden's gaze automatically followed. The head injury Dean had mentioned hadn't been obvious, but his stride, though rapid and purposeful, was uneven.

A little less put together than when he left…

With that memory, the rest of Dean's words echoed in her head, as well. *Served his country… Last tour… Hero.*

Maybe in her desperation to put an end to the nightmare the Nolans and this community were experiencing, she'd jumped to the wrong conclusion. The guy seemed sincere. And sincerely frustrated by the way she'd interpreted his story.

"You have to understand that *anybody* coming in here claiming to have seen Raine—"

Almost at the door, he turned sharply on his heel. "Oh, I understand. Believe me. Blame my naiveté about how investigations like this are handled for not getting the message before. I stupidly thought those requests for information—any information—were genuine. I guess you were just casting the wider net for suspects. I'm sorry I stumbled into it. You know where to find me if you have further questions."

He pushed through the narrow doorway without touching the two officers who were still standing frozen on either side.

In the silence that fell after Underwood's pronouncement, the three of them listened as his limping footsteps faded down the tiled hallway. A few seconds later the outside door slammed shut.

Only then did Eden make eye contact with her deputy chief. "I blew it, didn't I?"

Dean laughed. "I'd say your interrogation skills might need a little polishing."

He didn't seem upset about what had just happened, but then Dean hadn't believed from the beginning that Underwood had any hand in the kidnapping. Neither had Winton.

And reviewing the interview in her mind, she could understand their reservations about considering the ex-soldier a suspect. Despite her own preconceived notions, his reaction to her suggestion had rung true. As Dean had said about Ray Nolan, if Underwood was hiding something, he was a consummate actor. The problem wasn't that she'd had suspicions. Any law-enforcement officer would have, hearing his story secondhand. The problem was in the way she'd handled the face-to-face.

"I imagine the guys from the Bureau are going to be ticked off," she acknowledged.

"You gonna tell 'em about this?"

"You think I *shouldn't?*"

"I think they'll react the same way you just did. But if you believe that's what you ought to do…" Dean shrugged.

"I don't think I can legitimately keep Underwood's story from them. Do you?"

"*Major* Underwood."

An officer. Something she should have gleaned from his attitude, if nothing else.

"*Do* you?" Even as she repeated the question, Eden recognized that, in this case, calling the Bureau might fall under the category of "covering your ass." If she didn't pass this information on to the FBI, and something eventually came of it, she'd be considered derelict in her duty. The same word Jake Underwood had just used, she realized.

I thought it was my duty...

"Up to you, Chief," Dean said, refusing to let her off the hook. "For what it's worth, I don't think it makes a hill of beans difference *what* you do. I don't think Jake had anything to do with that little girl's disappearance. But I also think he can probably hold his own with the Feds. After all, he's been dealing with bureaucratic red tape most of his life. I suspect he'll be more than a match for the boys from Jackson."

Dean sounded as if he was enjoying the thought of that confrontation. The realization that he had no doubt how Underwood would handle himself should have been comforting, given that she felt she had little choice about sharing this information with the agents. If the ex-soldier thought *she'd* hassled him...

Eden blew out a breath, the frustrations of the past two days suddenly catching up with her. She needed a couple of hours sleep to go along with the partially eaten sandwich. Maybe then she could get some perspective back.

They'd done everything they could think of to find Raine Nolan. The feeling that it wasn't nearly enough was compounded by the realization that, despite the horror she'd felt listening to Jake Underwood's "flashback," despite the ridiculousness of even considering the possibility that what he'd seen was real, that vision—or whatever it had been—was the most positive indication they had had yet that Raine might still be alive.

Chapter Three

"I just want to make certain I understand what the term means." Eden looked up to make sure the door to her office was securely closed, although she had already done that before she'd placed this call.

It was bad enough that her inquiry into Jake Underwood's medical condition felt like an invasion of privacy, she wasn't sure how others in the department would interpret her interest. Dean's dismissal of what the ex-soldier claimed to have seen had been swift and definite. In spite of that, she felt compelled to check with someone who had more expertise in these matters than either of them.

"Brain damage can mean a whole lot of different things," Dr. Ben Murphy said. "You're gonna have to be a little more specific if you want me to give you a medical opinion."

"I don't know what I want," she admitted.

Doc Murphy had been her father's physician as well as his friend. She trusted both his discretion and his judgment.

"Closed-head trauma?"

"I don't even know that. All I know is he was a soldier."

The silence on the other end of the line made her wonder if Doc, with his quick intellect and broad knowledge of this town, had already put it all together.

"This an official inquiry?" he asked finally.

"Nope. This is just me asking a trusted friend for some guidance."

"Fair enough. Generalities, then. That all right?"

"If that's all you got."

"Give and take, Eden. Give and take."

"Well, you got all I can give, so…I'll take whatever you'll offer."

"The brain's a delicate thing. It can be damaged by cumulative injuries, like a football player who has too many concussions during his career. Then you can get stuff like ALS, maybe years afterward. He doesn't know his brain's been hurt until it's too late."

"I don't think that's the case here."

"I didn't figure it was. In war, the injury is usually obvious. A blow or a concussive force from an explosion, resulting in an open or closed wound to the head."

"Which is worse?"

She could almost hear Doc shrug. "Six of one, half a dozen of the other. It's the degree that matters. And the treatment, of course. In modern wars men survive things that would once have killed them, if not immediately, then within a matter of hours. Now sometimes within minutes, we get them off the battlefield and into a trauma unit that's as good, if not better, than most of those in our major hospitals. They relieve the pressure on the brain, maybe by removing a piece of the skull so it's got room to swell. Maybe with drugs. Whatever we'd do here, they can do there."

"And after that?"

"Depending on the damage, rehab to recover function."

"Function?"

"Mental and physical. I could do a better job of explaining this, Eden, if I had some clue as to what kind and degree of injury we're talking about."

"I can't help you with that. Just keep it general. So with this quick treatment, do most of them recover?"

"Some do. Some don't."

"And if they don't, what kinds of problems would they have?"

"Physically? You ever see somebody after a stroke? That's a kind of brain injury in itself. Muscle weakness, usually confined to one side of the body. Mentally? It could involve amnesia. Aphasia. Even personality changes."

The tip of the pencil she'd been jotting notes with lifted. "What kind?"

"Any kind. Somebody who's been mild-mannered and shy becomes overbearing. Or vice versa. Or they may suffer from extreme excitability. Impulsivity. Have anger-management issues."

"Might they become violent?"

Again there was a silence on the other end of the line. "It's possible. Anything's *possible,* Eden, but most of the men and women who suffer brain injuries come home and resume their lives. They may struggle with mobility or memory or control, but they don't become somebody else. If they weren't violent criminals before, most of them don't commit acts of violence after. They just come home and try to be the best they can be, despite what's happened to them while they were fighting on our behalf."

The silence this time was Eden's. She broke it finally to suggest, "I don't guess I need to tell you that I'd appreciate your keeping what we've talked about to yourself."

"You don't need to tell me. But I'd do it anyway. As on edge as folks in this town are right now, the suggestion that we've got somebody around here who's become dangerous because he's had a brain injury could be disastrous. Frankly, I wouldn't want that on my conscience."

"Thanks, Doc. I appreciate your help. *And* the advice."

"Your daddy would be proud of you, Eden. You're doing a good job. And the hardest one you got facing you may be keeping the yahoos here from going off the deep end. I'd hate to see that happen in Waverly."

"Me, too, Doc. Me, too."

"While you're taking care of everything else around here," the old man said, "don't forget to take care of you. We need you. Your daddy knew that, too."

"Thank, Doc. That means a lot."

"You just do what he taught you. You'll be fine.

YOU'RE A DAMNED slow learner, boy, Jake thought, as he watched the special agents' car disappear behind the cloud of dust that enveloped any vehicle exiting his property this time of year. Or maybe he was as brain-damaged as the surgeons who'd worked on him had feared he might be.

No matter the impetus, going to the police department had been a colossally stupid, totally idiotic mistake. One he still couldn't believe he'd made. And now that blonde Barbie, who hadn't believed a word he'd said, had sicced the Feds on him.

The old adages were true. Never volunteer. Keep your head down and do your job. Mind your own business.

That's exactly what he'd do from now on, Jake vowed. Even if he had another of what the agents had called "his visions."

Not that he planned on doing that. At least not the kind he'd had yesterday.

He had enough ghosts in his head already. He didn't need Raine Nolan's there, too.

BY THE END of Day Three, the effects of being overextended were apparent on everybody in the department. And probably on most of the townspeople as well, Eden acknowledged. The local search parties had been joined by teams with cadaver dogs—an unwelcome reality check, based on the passage of time since the Nolan child had been taken.

"You talk to the lab?" Dean asked.

"Yesterday *and* today. Special Agent Davis called them,

too. They say they're doing the best they can. And, truth be told, I'm not sure we sent them anything that's going to tell us much."

Cliff Davis was the senior of the two agents the Mississippi Bureau of Investigation had sent down. Eden had found him helpful and professional, but a couple of times, she thought she'd detected a gleam of contempt in his eyes when she asked for his opinion of things the department had talked about doing.

Paranoid, she chided herself. Everybody was grasping at straws, including the Bureau.

She'd been open with her officers, that if they had any ideas about other avenues they should be pursuing in this investigation, they should speak up. Several had, and they'd already put a couple of those suggestions into play.

And of course, they were still concentrating on the tried-and-true. They'd interviewed the registered sex offenders in the region—at least the ones they could track down. They'd also canvassed the upscale neighborhood where the Nolans lived to see if anyone had seen or heard anything unusual, not only on the night of the kidnapping, but also in the days leading up to it.

The Nolans had both taken lie-detector tests, verifying hers and Dean's initial reactions to their stories. The hotline and the Amber Alert had yielded a ton of calls, but so far nothing that led anywhere. Other than that…

"We sent 'em all we got." Dean's comment was nothing but the truth. A truth that grew less palatable with each passing hour.

"I don't know what else to do."

"You've done everything you can," her deputy chief said earnestly. "Nobody could'a handled this better. I mean that, Chief."

He always called her chief, despite how long he'd known

her. Almost twenty years, Eden realized, a little surprised it had been that long.

But then, her existence before they'd moved to Waverly seemed very distant. Another time. Another place. Another life.

"I really appreciate your saying that, Dean. I keep thinking there must be *something* we haven't thought of. Something that will give us a handle on who did this."

"Sometimes, despite all you can do, things like this just don't have a happy ending."

"I know." She did. The chance that they'd find Raine Nolan alive decreased hour by hour. And far too many of those had already passed.

"Why don't you go on home and get some sleep? I grabbed a few hours this morning. I can hold down the fort for a while."

Eden glanced at the clock above her office door. The windowless room made it too easy to lose track of time, especially when things had been as hectic as today. Still, she was surprised to find it was almost seven. It would be dark in another hour. Since the marshy terrain was too treacherous to risk after nightfall, even the search parties would be coming in.

She might as well take advantage of Dean's offer. He was more than capable of taking charge of the command center. *Especially when there was so little to command.*

"I think I'll do that. You'll call me if anything happens? And I mean anything, Dean."

"You'll be the first to know."

They both understood how unlikely such a call would be, given the end of the searching day. Sadly, it was now almost a relief when they had reached that point without incident. It meant that at least for one more day Eden didn't have to face Margo Nolan with the news that her daughter had been found. And that, against her mother's hopeful expectations, she wouldn't be coming home again.

HIS GRANDMOTHER USED to preach to him about "speaking things into existence." At the time, Jake had considered it all a bunch of Holy Roller hogwash, but when the familiar flickering began, his vow that he would keep any other "visions" to himself came to mind.

That was the last thought he managed before the horror closed in, so strong it made rational thinking impossible. The darkness was terrifying enough, but now, somehow, he knew what it contained. And understood the things that could happen within it.

He could again hear water dripping. Could smell its stench. Maybe if he opened his eyes…

There was more light this time, so that his surroundings were clearer, more distinct. Exposed roots lay against the black walls like a network of veins.

A trickle of moisture glinted on the ground in front of him, reflecting a light whose source he couldn't determine. The sun? Or something artificial? Something put into this place to illuminate it?

Not that it did. Not to any real degree.

A splinter of his mind continued to worry over that. The rest was lost in the same primitive fear that had encompassed him before.

This time, however, he knew something about the source of that fear. Not enough to identify it, but enough to know it was to be avoided at all costs.

Stooping, he scrambled backward to get away from it. Away from the light, he realized, which must mean—

As quickly as he'd been thrust into the darkness, he was thrown out of it. This time, rather than kneeling beside his truck, he was lying on the floor of his grandmother's parlor, the fibers of its faded wool carpet rough against his cheek.

Physically unable to move, he lay there for what seemed like hours, trying to orient himself into the present. When he had, he realized that, once again, where the flashback had taken him hadn't been to the past. Not back to the desert. Not the war.

This had been something more immediate. Something nearer in both time and space.

He hadn't seen the little girl. He searched the fragments of memory that lingered like smoke in his brain and found within them no trace of another presence.

He'd been the only one there. In the darkness. And whoever was coming…

Whoever.

Not whatever. Whoever. His subconscious had known that before he had consciously arrived at the phrase.

Whoever was coming…

He pushed up from the floor, feeling as if he'd been physically beaten. The flashbacks always left him dazed, almost hungover. This…this was something different. An alternative unpleasantness.

He'd been terrified again. A sick, bowel-tightening horror that revolved around whoever was going to appear out of that darkness. Despite the long years of his military career, through all the firefights and ambushes he'd survived, he couldn't remember ever being that frightened.

Because there's nothing you can do about what's going to happen.

That was it exactly. Always before, he had felt that, no matter what they threw at him, he could hold his own. Maybe he would die, but if he did, it would be while giving as good as he got.

That wasn't how he had felt crouching in that clammy darkness. He'd felt helpless. Far worse than that, he realized, he'd felt hopeless.

He took a breath, mentally fighting the return of those emotions. He put his forearm on the coffee table, using its support to push to his knees.

He waited for the room to steady before he got painfully

to his feet. He had no recollection of how he'd ended up face-down on the carpet. No recollection even of why he'd been in this room.

He eased down on the couch, resisting the urge to lower his head into his hands. As much as he had hated the loss of control the flashbacks had represented, their horrific violence now seemed almost safe. Familiar. His.

The other wasn't. And his reaction to whatever was happening there…wasn't his reaction.

That realization was as unnerving as the reaction itself. The fact that he was somehow attuned to the feelings of the little girl he had glimpsed out of the corner of his eye.

By now he'd studied every newspaper photograph of Raine Nolan, memorizing the smiling face on the flyers that blanketed the town. And he still couldn't decide if the child he'd seen cowering in that darkness was her.

Except, who else could it be? The timing of this, if nothing else, argued that whatever he'd experienced during the past three days must be connected to her abduction.

Or to the fact that somebody blew a good-size chuck of your brain to smithereens.

Had Eden Reddick's question about whether there'd been someone else in the pit with the girl planted that notion in his head? Had his mind latched on to the suggestion, so that this time he'd imagined there was someone else there?

Angry with the possibility, he tried to stand. The resulting vertigo made him clutch the arm of the couch until the room righted itself.

He wasn't crazy, he told himself fiercely. Maybe what was happening to him fell into that category, but *he* didn't. And he wasn't going to pretend he did, not to satisfy Reddick or anyone else.

Somewhere a terrified child was hiding in a darkness she didn't understand. Hiding in fear from a horror she was only beginning to comprehend.

Through some quirk of a cruel universe, he'd been allowed to know that. To feel what she felt.

And now, no matter the cost, it was up to him to figure out what he could do about it.

Chapter Four

It's on my way home, Eden justified as she pulled off the highway and onto the dirt road. *And I'll sleep better if I make sure.*

Since she'd had a hard time keeping her eyes open during the last hour she'd spent at the office, that rationalization was an even bigger stretch than the "on my way" detour she'd just made. It was true, however, that this had been all she'd thought of as she'd tried to come up with anything they hadn't checked out.

The caves at the end of this unpaved lane had played a role in the childhood of almost everyone who'd grown up in Waverly. And even in some who hadn't. She'd learned about them almost as soon as she and her dad moved here.

And they've probably been searched a dozen times since Raine's kidnapping. Still, since she herself hadn't asked anyone from the department to do that, she needed to make certain it had been done.

It was only as she was climbing out of the car to begin the trek up the slope to the rocks above that she admitted the real reason she was here. The caves best fit the description Jake Underwood had given from his "vision."

Like the Nolans, the ex-soldier had passed a voluntary lie-detector test. And the background check the Bureau had done revealed a service record impressive enough to merit the initial description of him that Winton and Dean had used.

Despite that, both the agents and her deputy chief had discounted Underwood's story as being nothing more than the result of his head injury. After all, to think anything else would open them up to a belief system far beyond the narrow limits of their own.

Apparently, however, not beyond mine, Eden admitted, as she struggled up the last few yards to the first cave's entrance. What was little more than a fissure in the face of the hillside hid a relatively large interior space. As she remembered it, the second nearby cavern was much smaller.

She waited a moment, giving her breathing a chance to steady. The sun was beginning to slip behind the rock face, casting the area where she stood into deep shadow.

She removed the flashlight from her utility belt, and then, the second motion more tentative than the first, her weapon from its holster. There was no telling what kind of wildlife might have taken refuge in the coolness of the cave.

Despite being armed with both a light and her Glock, still she hesitated, fighting a residual childhood fear of the dark she hadn't thought about in years.

Check it out and then go home. Get into bed and sleep until morning. Something she hadn't done since this case started.

She blew out a calming breath and then bent to slip though the crack. Once inside the cave, she directed the beam of her flashlight in a slow circle around its perimeter.

She could hear water dripping somewhere, its soft, regular plops the only sound in the rockbound stillness. She walked forward, redirecting her light, trying to locate the place where that moisture hit the floor. When she couldn't find that, she raised the beam, allowing it to play over the ceiling, which was higher than she'd remembered from her one hurried, adolescent visit.

They'd gone in on a dare, she and Margaret Eames, the only two in the group who'd never been inside the caves. She'd always wondered if Margaret shared her slight sense of claustrophobia, since neither of them had remained longer than required by the taunts of their classmates.

She made one last slow circuit of the cave with her light, reassuring herself there were no hidden areas where a child could be concealed. She'd do the same in the smaller and then go home and crash.

Only when she turned toward the entrance did she realize she wasn't alone. A dark shape obscured the narrow opening, blocking what little light had been coming in from outside.

She brought her weapon up, at the same time redirecting the focus of the flashlight. Jake Underwood flinched, lifting his hand to shield his eyes.

"Don't." Although Eden hadn't been certain about the intent of his movement when she'd barked that command, she *had* been sure that, despite whatever lingering disabilities his wounds had left, she was physically no match for the ex-soldier.

"Then shut off that damn light."

She didn't obey, asking instead, "What are you doing here?"

Her mind raced through the possibilities, forced to reject those that had to do with his keeping Raine prisoner. Not only had she verified the cave was empty, if Underwood *were* the kidnapper, he'd have to be an idiot to confront her.

Something else that his service record had disproved.

"The same thing you are."

Eden hesitated, knowing that if she admitted she'd been checking out a location that matched his "flashback," she would also be admitting that she'd given credence to that vision.

"Or am I wrong?" he asked into her silence.

"This is the only thing I could think of that we might not have covered."

"You mean the possibility that what I told you *did* have

something to do with the Nolan girl?" There was a trace of sarcasm in his question.

"Like I said, we've covered everything else." She sounded defensive, yet she was only doing what her father had taught her. Leave no stone unturned—no matter how unlikely. "Coming here falls under the category of grasping at straws, I guess."

He lowered his hand, his eyes apparently having adjusted to her light. "Sorry you went to the trouble, then. This isn't it."

"What?"

"This isn't where she's being held."

Present tense, Eden noted. For some reason, her tired spirit responded to that.

"You've searched the other one? The other cave?" Maybe while she'd been searching this one?

He shook his head. "It's not rock. I don't know why I didn't remember that until I came. Maybe I just didn't notice."

"Notice...?"

"Wherever she is—that place she's in—it's been dug out of the earth. I could see exposed roots in the dirt. Tree roots. The roots of shrubs. Just...no rock."

Eden realized that she had been listening with her lips parted, seemingly willing to take in every word the guy said. Angry with that eagerness to believe, she closed her mouth and then lowered the flashlight so that it was no longer directed at him.

"Which means it could be anywhere." She'd kept her tone flat, but he clearly read what she was feeling.

"Look, I don't care whether you believe me or not. All I'm telling you is this isn't the place." Despite the fact her weapon was still trained on his chest, Underwood turned, shrugging broad shoulders through the opening in the rock.

Did she believe that he'd just happened to think of these

caves and come to investigate? Or did he have some other, more sinister reason for being in this isolated location?

She shivered, unsure whether that thought or the natural chill of the cave was responsible. She listened, but couldn't hear any sounds that would indicate Underwood was moving down the trail. Which meant...

Taking a breath, she switched off her light and then ducked through the opening. As she straightened, she saw him standing at the head of the path, looking down the slope. The evening shadows had elongated, reaching into the trees below.

"I'll wait while you check the other one," he said without looking at her.

In spite of the heat, the insects had started their evening song. She actually debated taking his word for it that this wasn't the place before she turned and trudged up to the second cave. She didn't bother going inside, simply directing her flashlight around the interior.

Nothing there. Just as she'd expected.

And just as he'd told her.

She switched off her light and realized only then that she still held her weapon. She shoved the Glock back into its holster, turning as she did to look at the ex-soldier. He hadn't moved, his continued stillness unnerving.

"If the caves aren't what you saw—" she began.

"She could be anywhere. Anywhere isolated enough that he could dig a hole and lower her into it without anyone seeing him."

The despair in his voice echoed what she had felt all day. They were well beyond any time frame in which conventional wisdom suggested a kidnap victim might still be alive. And they were no closer to finding Raine than they had been when the 911 call came in.

"He?" She had finally grasped the significant part of what Underwood had just said.

"She's terrified… It doesn't seem like a woman could produce that level of fear."

"But if she's alone and in the dark—"

"It's more than that. It's him."

It would be, of course. As she and Dean had speculated that first morning, whoever had taken Raine hadn't done it for money.

You're acting as if this guy knows what he's talking about. As if he really is tuned into that little girl's terror.

"If I were you, I wouldn't say something like that to anyone in town."

He turned, his eyes hard. "I did what I was told to do and look where it got me. Believe me, I'm not likely to talk up my 'insanity' around town. You ready?"

Should she consider his determination not to leave her alone up here a vestige of his upbringing or something more sinister? Except she hadn't gotten that vibe from him. After the initial spurt of fear, she hadn't been afraid to be alone with him. She wasn't now.

And there was nothing else to examine up here. Another dead end. Another in a long, frustrating series of them.

"I'm ready."

She had expected him to let her lead the way, but he started down the trail, leaving her to follow. As she did, she realized that she wouldn't have been comfortable with him trailing behind her through the growing darkness. And he had known that.

Just as he'd known why she was out here? Hell, maybe he *was* psychic.

Or maybe you've gone way too many hours without sleep.

They didn't speak again until they reached her cruiser. She opened the door and then hesitated. In the gathering twilight, he had watched her every move.

She met his eyes, deciding that, since she'd come this far, she might as well go all the way. In for a penny…

"You think she's still alive?"

He didn't answer for a long heartbeat, his eyes focusing on something up the slope behind her. When he looked at her again, he shook his head. "I don't have any reason to believe she isn't."

"Then…?"

"I can't tell you anything else. Maybe if there's another one…"

She nodded as if that made sense. Maybe it did. At least as much as any other avenue they'd pursued. She'd already bent, ready to slip into the driver's seat, when he spoke again.

"Thanks."

"For what?"

"For coming out here. For going that far."

"You'd be surprised how far I'd go to find Raine Nolan."

"Because it's your job?"

My duty…

"That's part of it." That and the memory of another little girl no one had found.

"And the rest?"

"Like you said. She's terrified." Alone and in the dark with a madman. "Unless *somebody* finds her…"

Eden left the sentence unfinished. They both knew the reality. A reality most of the people working on this case had already conceded. That she hadn't, she realized, had as much to do with this man than with any claim she might make about duty.

"If you do…have another one, I mean…" Again her words trailed.

Underwood nodded. "Yeah. Yeah, I will."

He was still standing on the edge of the dirt road when she had turned the car and headed back down it. In the darkness his silhouette seemed to merge with the woods behind him. She slowed, pushing the button that would lower the window on the passenger side.

"Where's your car?"

"Truck. There's a turnoff a few feet back." He gestured with his head in the direction she'd just come.

Her eyes lifted to the rearview mirror. She hadn't seen another road, but then she'd only been looking for a place wide enough to turn the patrol car. Obviously, he knew this area better than she did. Well enough to know where to conceal his truck.

She dismissed that flicker of doubt, remembering the sincerity in his voice when he'd talked about Raine. "It's going to be dark soon."

There didn't seem to be any reason for him to stay out here, but he didn't appear to be headed to his truck. Was it possible he was feeling the effects of that climb?

Impulsively, she acted on that thought. "If you want to get in, I can back up to wherever you're parked."

His eyes lifted to briefly consider the road behind her before they came back to meet hers. "I may look around. Since I'm here. I didn't see this area on any of the search grids."

She hadn't either, so that part made sense. Except what did he think he was going to be able to see in the dark?

"It's gonna be hard to see up here pretty soon," she reminded him with a smile.

The one he gave in response emphasized the shape of his mouth, its bottom lip fuller than she'd noticed before. She was shocked at the flutter of desire in her lower body.

"I like the dark."

The unease generated by that statement negated the attraction she'd just felt. And it wasn't as easy to dismiss as had been his familiarity with this locale. After all, Dean said he'd spent summers here growing up.

"Okay, then. Just be careful. I don't think we have the manpower to mount another search and rescue."

"I'll keep that in mind." He touched the roof of the car as

if in dismissal and then turned to walk toward the path they'd just descended.

Eden eased her foot off the brake, directing her car down the narrow track. When she raised her eyes again to the rear-view mirror, Jake Underwood had already disappeared into the forest.

Chapter Five

The peal of the phone pulled her out of a sleep so deep she was drugged by it. It took a moment for her to realize what the sound was. Another to find the receiver in the pitch-darkness of her bedroom.

"Hello?"

"You probably ought to come on in to the office." Dean's voice lacked its customary thread of good humor.

"They found her."

"No. Sorry. Nothing like that."

"Then what?"

"Folks are stirred up about the Underwood thing. I just think you might want to be here."

The Underwood thing. Despite the events of last night, it took a second for her to realize what her deputy chief was talking about.

"How the hell did they find out?"

"It's Waverly, Eden. How do you think?"

Calling her by her first name was a sign of Dean's agitation. He hadn't done that since the day her daddy had pinned the chief's badge on her uniform shirt.

"If somebody in the department talked, they're done. I don't care who it is."

"Yeah, well, you can fire 'em later. Right now, you need to get your butt out of bed and come down here."

"They're at the *station?*" She glanced at the alarm clock, surprised to find it was only a little past nine—less than an hour after she'd fallen into bed. No wonder she felt drugged.

"Demanding we bring him in. When we don't, it's gonna get ugly."

"Damn it. When I get my hands on whoever—"

"Like I said, Chief, later."

"You talk to them. They'll believe you before they will me."

The sudden silence left her wondering what she was missing. Had Dean already tried that? Or…was it possible he thought they were right?

"Dean?"

"Yeah. I'll tell 'em what the Feds told us, but they're gonna want to talk to you."

"I'll be there in ten minutes. Just keep them calm until then."

"*Keep* 'em calm? You're making a hell of an assumption."

"Just hold on until I get there."

IT DIDN'T TAKE long for Eden to realize Dean hadn't exaggerated. A dozen men crowded into the confines of the conference room where Winton had taken Jake Underwood. Although Dean was trying to keep order, they were clearly past the point of being reasoned with.

"What's going on here?" she shouted over the hubbub as she took her place beside him. It quieted them, if only momentarily.

"You protecting Underwood. That's what's going on."

Eden didn't see who'd said that, but the chorus of agreement indicated it didn't matter. They were apparently of one accord.

"The agents from the MBI—"

"If somebody's crazy, they may believe what they're saying

enough to fool a machine," the same voice called out. "That ain't to say the bastard didn't take her."

She hadn't expected the results of the lie-detector test to be completely negated by Underwood's wounds. She was beginning to appreciate what Dean had been dealing with.

"He says he saw her," Lincoln Greene said from the front. "That he knows where she is. That doesn't alarm you?"

Greene was the owner of the local hardware store. And not known as a hothead. There was no denying that he was hot right now.

"Major Underwood has flashbacks. We believe that—"

"Yeah, a flashback to when he took her. You asked him where the place is that he saw? You ask him that, Chief?"

"Actually, I talked to Major Underwood this afternoon." This time she raised her voice to continue speaking over the resulting mutter. "I can assure you that neither this department nor the Federal agents assigned to this case believe he has anything to do with the kidnapping."

"Then why'd you meet with him?" Greene demanded.

A chorus of "yeah's" followed. She held up her hand, palm forward. "We both ended up at the same location while searching for Raine. I can promise you that Major Underwood is as concerned about that little girl as any of us. He was out looking for her. Just as all of you have been."

The couple of seconds of silence that followed that reminder was enough to make her believe she'd talked some sense into them. At least, until Reilly Dawson piped up.

"You sure he wasn't just revisiting the scene of the crime like they say murderers do? You look for blood around there, Chief?"

"Since we have no reason to believe Raine Nolan is dead," Eden said evenly, "I wasn't there to look for blood. I was out there to look for a child. A living child. So was Major Underwood."

"That ain't what the news is saying." Dave Porter was a

shade-tree mechanic, one good enough to service the department's cars as well as most of the watercraft in the area. "They're saying that, after all this time, chances are good she's dead. They're saying y'all are just looking for her body now."

"Well, they're wrong," Eden said. "We're still looking for Raine. And that's exactly what you should be using all this energy for, instead of accusing somebody who's been cleared by both the MBI and the FBI."

Another moment of quiet, broken by Greene's question. "Then how do you explain what he says he saw? That vision, or whatever it was?"

"I don't explain it. I can't. I just don't believe he had anything to do with the kidnapping."

"But you do believe he saw where she is?"

The delay before she answered was too long. Inherently honest, Eden was no longer sure what she believed. Only what Jake Underwood did.

"Is that why the two of you met up today? You out looking for the place he described and just 'ran into him' so to speak?"

Paul Springfield's sarcasm was broad enough to generate laughter and a few catcalls.

"That don't make you wonder?" Porter reiterated.

"What makes me wonder is why you all are wasting this time and furor on something that I'm telling you isn't related. I've told you what we know to be fact. Now you all need to go on home, get a good night's sleep, and get up in the morning and help the search parties. We'll be making assignments for those at eight a.m., the same as we do every day. I'll expect to see all of you back here then. If not, then I'll know exactly what y'all are really interested in. And it isn't in finding Raine Nolan."

Nobody broke this silence. Not until Dean said, "Now go on. Get out of here. You've wasted enough of everybody's time with this nonsense."

Several of the men began to turn toward the door, the heat suddenly seeming to evaporate in the face of their combined demands. Greene didn't move, holding Eden's eyes.

"This isn't over, you know. I don't know why you're protecting that bastard, but when it all comes out, you better realize that you won't be able to do that anymore. Not when they find that little girl."

"Go home," Dean ordered, putting his hand on the man's shoulder to turn him. "This is done. This *and* your threats."

Greene didn't resist, but he jerked out the deputy chief's hold, pushing his way through the knot of men near the door. Only when the room had cleared did Eden release the breath she hadn't realized she'd been holding.

"He's right about one thing," Dean said.

"What's that?"

"They aren't finished with this. The longer she's missing, the more eager they're gonna be to take their frustrations out on somebody. Right now, the only available target seems to be Underwood."

JAKE HAD NO IDEA what had awakened him. No memory of a sound or a dream or anything else that would pull him out of the restless sleep he'd finally, long after he'd gone to bed, fallen into. All he knew was that every instinct, developed through years of training and experience, told him he needed to be awake. And vigilant.

As his gaze swept slowly across the moon-touched landscape of his grandmother's farm, he couldn't find a shadow out of place. There wasn't a whisper of sound, other than the ones that lulled him to sleep every night. Not a flicker of movement.

Still, something was wrong. Every hair on the back of his neck was raised, his well-honed sense of danger in full operational mode.

He turned his head, his eyes searching the narrow porch

that ran across the front of the house. Nothing. And since he'd come out through the window of his bedroom, which was at the back, he knew there was no one there, either.

Still…

Jake's fingers automatically tightened around his grandfather's rifle, his heart rate reacting to the sudden spurt of adrenaline. He watched as a shadow, minutely darker than its surroundings, drifted along the perimeter of the property.

Despite his leg, Jake moved soundlessly to the other side of the small toolshed he'd hidden behind, attempting to get an angle on whoever was out there.

A cloud obscured the moon, causing him to glance up. It was large enough that the intruder should be able to use it to reach the grove of pines that flanked the pasture. And once there…

Once there, he realized, whoever was out here would be concealed from view until they came out on the other side of the house. He could watch until that happened, or—

The slight smile that tugged at the corner of his lips had nothing to do with whatever was happening now and a whole hell of a lot to do with what had gone on during the last eighteen months. He was already moving before it faded.

NOT EXACTLY ON her way home, Eden conceded. And it had taken her a couple of hours, after the confrontation with the townspeople, to get away from the station.

However, she hadn't been able to reach Jake Underwood on the number he had provided to the department, and she wouldn't be able to sleep unless she warned him about what had happened tonight.

She closed her cell in frustration and ducked her head so she could see out of the side window. Although it had been a while since she'd been out here, she seemed to remember the driveway to the Wells' place sneaked up on you. Almost before the thought had formed, she was forced to slam on her brakes to make the turn.

As soon as she pulled off the two-lane, she saw there was a truck parked on the verge, just at the entrance of the long drive. She pulled in behind it, killing her lights.

She sat there for a moment, letting her eyes adjust to the darkness. The tree frogs were the only sound in the nighttime stillness as she tried to figure out what the hell was going on here.

Jake Underwood had corrected her when she'd asked about his car, so it was always possible this was *his* truck. But if so, why was it parked so far from the house?

She couldn't come up with a plausible explanation. Not one that bode well for the occupant of the farmhouse, which, bathed in moonlight, lay a good five hundred yards from where she was sitting.

Remembering the anger that had filled the crowded conference room, she opened the door of the cruiser and stepped out. The night creatures were louder outside the car, but instead of closing her door, she eased it shut without engaging the lock.

Then she surveyed the scene in front of her. Nothing moved. It all seemed as bucolic as an English countryside. As safe as she would have proclaimed Waverly to be four days ago.

She skirted the vehicle in front of hers, taking time to cup her hand against the driver's side window to peer inside. Nothing there to identify the owner. And although its plates were from this county, she didn't recognize the truck.

She straightened, again looking at the distant house. There might be a perfectly innocent explanation for why the driver had parked at the top of the long drive, but the ones that came to mind right now weren't.

She pressed the button on her shoulder radio and, as softly as she could, said into it, "I need you to run a tag." She shined her utility light on the license plate. "FRD-eight four six. Dark blue Ford 150. Older model, but I don't know the year." She waited until the dispatcher had repeated the information. "Don't respond to me when you get it. I'll call you back when I can."

She unsnapped the holster of her weapon and lifted it out. The cool, solid feel of its butt against her palm was reassuring, despite the adrenaline that had already begun flooding her body.

She blew out a breath and drew in another. Then she began to move, running toward the stand of pines that lay to the west of the homestead.

Once there, she stopped to reconnoiter. Nothing seemed out of place. Nothing—

The arm that snaked around her waist lifted her off her feet. As she was crushed against a chest that felt as solid as oak, her gun was stripped from her hand.

Like taking candy from a baby.

The realization infuriated her. She kicked back with her right foot, the heel of her boot making a satisfying contact with the shin of whoever held her. At the same time, she twisted, trying to free herself.

"Stop it," the man who'd captured her growled against her ear. "It's me. Underwood."

Intent on her struggles, it took a second for that identification to sink in.

Before it did, as if to emphasize his command, he shook her, hard enough to make her teeth snap together. "Stop it or you're going to get us both killed."

His breath was warm on her cheek. The stubble she'd noticed the night he'd come to the station moved against her skin. Abrasive. Highly masculine. As unreasonable as it seemed, given the situation, she felt that same rush of sexual awareness she'd experienced this afternoon.

"Okay," she whispered. "Okay."

He waited a heartbeat and then set her on her feet. She began to turn, but staggered slightly under the force of the flight-or-fight response that had flooded her body when he grabbed her. His hand fastened under her elbow to steady her.

She shook it off, completing the turn so that she faced him. She could barely make out his features, their hard angles sinister in the darkness. "What are you doing out here?"

"I *live* here, remember?" He held out her gun, which she took automatically.

He hadn't asked why *she* was here, but after all, that was what she'd come to tell him. "Somehow people in town found out what you told us. Some of them…some of them think you must have had something to do with the kidnapping."

He didn't question how they'd found out. He didn't question anything at all. He simply took her elbow again and began pulling her along with him.

"What are you doing?"

"Shh…"

He didn't slow, despite his limp. Nor did he look at her. And unless she wanted him to literally drag her, she had no choice but to try to keep up.

Chapter Six

He finally stopped at the edge of the woods, propping his left shoulder against the trunk of a pine to look around it toward the house. Then he stepped to the other side of the tree in that same slow survey.

"What are you planning to do?" she whispered.

"What do you think?"

Eden knew every one of the men who'd been in the conference room tonight. And their families. Even if they were in the wrong, she couldn't let him conduct some kind of commando raid against them.

A raid like the one they were conducting?

"I think handling this is my job."

He turned, finally looking at her. "Whoever's out there didn't come to make a social call."

"I know." She did. She had intended to warn him of exactly that possibility. "But if you go after them with the intent to kill...then *you're* the one on the wrong side of the law."

"They're on my property. At night. By now, they may even be inside my house. That's where they were headed, the last time I saw them."

Around here, breaking into someone's home at night was a good way to get your head blown off, especially when you considered the percentage of the population who owned guns.

Normally, few questions would be asked if that happened. Not even by law enforcement. In this case...

"If Raine Nolan isn't found soon, these men aren't the only ones who are going to start wondering about what you told us. You don't want to provide fuel for that speculation by doing something stupid."

He appeared to at least think about what she'd said. "And what are *you* planning to do? Tell them to come out with their hands up?"

"Something like that. It *is* my job." She and Dean had been able to quell the mob mentality at the station. Maybe she could do that again.

And maybe you're the one who's going to get your head blown off.

"They pay you enough to take that kind of risk?"

"They *pay* me to uphold the law. Stay here." She wasn't about to hang around until he, or her own better judgment, changed her mind.

Holding her weapon extended in front of her in both hands, she walked toward the house. She knew these men. They were family men. Churchgoers. Law-abiding citizens of the town she had sworn to protect. They weren't going to risk everything by going off half-cocked.

"Hello, in the house. This is Chief Reddick." Although her voice sounded strong, she was feeling more foolish—and more vulnerable—by the second.

There was no answer. She glanced back to where she'd left Jake. If he was still there, he was concealed by the shadows beneath the trees. She turned to face the darkened farmhouse.

"Whatever you think you're doing, you need to stop and consider your families. Come on out now and let's talk. Just like we did at the station."

Probably the best she could hope for was if whoever had driven into Jake's driveway took this opportunity to exit the rear of the house and return to his truck. And as far as what she would do about this incident tomorrow...

She realized that was probably the sticking point for who-ever was inside: what the repercussions of tonight's stunt would be.

"So far, nobody's been hurt," she began again, wondering how far she could go in suggesting this could be resolved without charges being filed. A lot of that would be up to the man waiting behind her. A man who seemed to be spoiling for a fight. "As long as we keep it that way—"

She felt the bullet brush by her cheek before she heard the report of the gun that fired it. Then something hit her around the knees, bringing her down hard even as the second shot sounded.

She raised her head to watch as Jake Underwood rolled off her. He stayed low, the rifle he'd carried trained on the house.

"I don't think they're much interested in talking." He didn't look at her, seeming to concentrate instead on his target.

Despite the sting of his mockery, she knew he was right. Whoever had come out here in the middle of the night to invade his home wouldn't believe they could get away with it. This had gone too far, which apparently everyone but she had already realized.

"You coming or staying?" he asked over his shoulder.

"You can't just—"

"What if they brought gasoline with them? I'm not going to sit here and wait for them to burn my grandmother's home to the ground. You coming or not?"

She could sense his tension, like a spring that had been wound too tight. "Coming," she affirmed finally.

"Then stay close. And don't go off on your own."

After getting shot at, that was unlikely. She thought she was ready to move, but when he exploded into motion, she had to scramble to keep up.

His limping run zigzagged across the yard. As she struggled to follow it exactly, she realized he was taking advantage of every shadow, every bush that offered concealment. Winded, she stopped behind him at one of those, as he again examined the moonlit house.

"There's an open window at the back." His eyes flicked down to her face as he whispered the information. "We go in there."

She nodded, at the same time wondering if she could talk him out of this. Or if she wanted to.

Whatever the result of Jake's actions, whoever was inside his house had started this confrontation. And shooting at the Chief of Police was pretty much understood to put you on the wrong side of any situation.

Then Jake was on the move again, forcing her to run to keep up.

As he worked his way around to the back of the house, sticking to the shadows, Jake considered the information Eden Reddick had just given him. He should have known that what he'd told her would become public knowledge. And that as soon as it did, he would become the prime suspect in the eyes of the town.

Even so, he wouldn't have expected what was happening out here tonight. An angry crowd calling him out, maybe. But a nighttime raid? Shots fired at a woman?

In spite of Eden's title, that's how he thought of her. Despite the starched precision of the uniform she wore, she was still very *much* a woman.

Because of that, his every instinct had been to protect her. Which complicated the hell out of what was going on.

He had reached the far corner of the house, so he stopped, shielding his body as he peered around it. The backyard looked peaceful in the moonlight. The only movement was the occasional flutter of the aged lace curtain at the window he'd crawled out of.

He looked over his shoulder to find Eden pressed against the wall behind him, her hands still wrapped around her weapon. He shook his head to indicate that he couldn't see anyone, and she nodded her understanding.

If he could be sure that whoever had fired those shots was inside, he'd leave her out here. Convince her to be lookout or something. The trouble was he couldn't be sure.

It made no sense for whoever this was to hang around, now that the authorities were here. Of course, it hadn't made much sense for them to shoot at those authorities, either.

Amateurs, he reminded himself. New to the world of stalking people rather than animals. A description that, unfortunately for them, didn't apply to him.

"I'm going in," he whispered, again turning to gauge her reaction.

Her mouth opened, drawing his eyes. The parted lips looked as if they were waiting for his kiss. He felt a wave of need and desire disproportionate to that unintended provocation.

Too damn long without a woman, he acknowledged. He'd probably have responded to any woman he was this close to.

So close he could smell her. Her hair maybe. Something floral. Sweet. Clean. And underlying that, the sharp, unmistakable scent of fear.

"Stay right behind me. I mean that."

She nodded, her throat working as she swallowed.

Fighting the urge to reassure her, he turned around to make a final scan of their surroundings before he left his position. At the back of the yard, almost to the distant line of trees, something moved.

He raised his weapon to his shoulder. As he tracked the shadowy shape, the woman behind him reached out and pulled the barrel down.

"He's leaving."

"How the hell do you know what he's doing?" Furious, he jerked the rifle out of her hold.

"It doesn't matter. He's not inside your house."

"*He's* not. But someone else may be." He rounded the corner and, back pressed against the wall, edged toward the window, marked in the darkness by that flutter of lace.

After a quick scan to determine the bedroom was empty, he put his leg over the sill and ducked inside. He sensed rather than felt Eden moving in behind him.

With a couple of strides, he crossed the bedroom and positioned himself by the door to the hall. When Eden slipped into place beside him, he put his arm across her body to push her back. His forearm inadvertently brushed her breasts, reawakening the desire he'd acknowledged outside.

He turned to mouth, "Stay here." Once more, she nodded to show that she understood.

Then he stepped into the hallway and began moving toward the front of the house. As he did, he made an effort to avoid the heart-pine floorboards that would creak under his weight.

His grandmother's front parlor was deserted. As was the connecting dining room. Beyond it, the refrigerator gleamed like a ghost in the moonlight.

The house was empty. He could feel it.

"I don't think—"

Startled, Jake whirled, automatically bringing up the rifle. Eden raised the muzzle of her own weapon, her knees bent as she assumed a shooter's stance.

A trained reaction to the threat of his gun? Or did she really believe he was crazy enough to shoot somebody who'd come out here to help him? "I thought I told you to stay put."

Her eyes were wide in the darkness, but she didn't apologize for her gaffe. "I don't think there's anyone inside."

"If there was, there isn't now." He deliberately lowered the rifle. After a second or two, she did the same, allowing the Glock to fall to her side.

"I called in the tags on the truck out front. I didn't know if it was yours, but I couldn't figure out why you'd park so far from the house."

That's what had awakened him, he realized. Either the sound of the engine or the lights, as somebody pulled into the drive.

"Mine's in the garage." At least it had been when he'd gone to bed.

"This one's out by the road. A dark blue Ford."

He shook his head, trying to imagine someone being stupid enough to park in his driveway while they attempted a raid on his property. Amateurs, he thought again, almost amused this time.

"They should have the ownership information by now." She pressed the button of the radio on her shoulder, identifying herself before asking for the results of the trace she'd initiated.

He could tell that she didn't like what she was hearing.

"Are you sure?" she asked. And then, "Thanks, Dean." And after another response. "I'll let you know when I leave."

She released the button, raising her eyes to his. "One of our upstanding local citizens."

"That's a pretty obvious calling card for a nighttime raid."

"He didn't have any way to know I'd be coming out here. Or anybody else, for that matter. Your place is pretty isolated."

That was true enough, but still, the idiocy of the mischief-maker parking his car in the driveway seemed almost cartoonish. Or maybe a little too convenient.

"And when you challenged him to come out and talk?"

She shrugged, apparently committed to making this work. "I think he figured it was too late by then."

She sounded almost too calm. Too rational. Somebody had just shot at her. Somebody she knew. Maybe even somebody she liked.

"You okay?" The question was out before he could stop it.

Whether she was or not wasn't his concern. As she'd said. She'd just been doing her job.

Hell, maybe somebody taking potshots at her was routine. Even as he thought that, he remembered where they were. His grandmother had never locked her doors. Not even at night.

"You think somebody's still out there? Or is it safe to turn on the lights?"

He weighed the wisdom of doing that, but some undercurrent in her voice made the decision for him. He headed toward the house's bathroom. It might be old-fashioned and cramped, but more important right now, it was windowless.

He pulled the chain on the globe over the medicine cabinet. When he turned, he realized why she'd made this request.

Blood streamed from a cut on her temple. At some point she'd rubbed it, smearing a streak of red across her cheek and into her hair.

His assessment was quick and certain. Not a bullet wound. She had probably struck her head on something when he'd taken her legs out from under her.

He stepped forward to grip her chin in his hand. Tilting her head into the light, he made the next conclusion as rapidly as he had the first. "This is going to need stitches."

She pulled free of his hold to look in the mirror, lifting the blood-stained hair away from the injury. "You have a Band-Aid?"

"Probably. But if you don't get it stitched, that will leave a scar."

She let her hair fall over the cut and turned to face him. "I have to meet Dean."

"Dean?"

"My chief deputy. He's going to Greene's house."

"Greene?" He felt like a fool, trying to keep up with the plot without knowing the cast.

"Lincoln Greene. That's his truck outside."

"And you think he's just going to go home and get into bed, like nothing's happened?"

"Where else *would* he go?"

She made it sound as if that action was the only one that made sense. Maybe in Waverly it was.

"Band-Aid?" she prodded.

He opened the door of the medicine cabinet, the space in the room so tight he had to lean across her to do so.

Suddenly he was physically aware of her again. Of her smell. Of the shape of her slender body. Of the fact that she was a woman.

And God knew, he needed one.

He fumbled with the Band-Aids he'd found, searching for the right size. When he had it, he closed the box and dropped it into the sink before he ripped the paper off the one he'd selected.

Then he hesitated, reluctant because of his growing attraction to touch her. Not even to play medic.

"I can do it." She reached out to take the bandage from his hand. Looking into the mirror, she began to position it over the abrasion.

"That needs to be cleaned first."

Her hands stilled. She turned to face him, eyes slightly widened.

Did she think he was deliberately trying to prolong this? To make some kind of move on her?

Would she be wrong?

Once more he reached across her, his fingers trembling as they closed around the dark brown bottle of peroxide. What the hell was wrong with him? Eden Reddick wasn't the only attractive female he'd ever been around. At one time, he'd actually been someone who was considered to know his way around women.

A lifetime ago.

He tipped the peroxide onto a cotton ball. "Hold still."

She obeyed, letting him dab at the cut until the broken skin foamed. When he began to clean up some of the smeared blood, she took the cotton from his hand.

He stepped back as, using the mirror to guide her, she completed the operation far more efficiently than his suddenly awkward hands would have allowed him to do. "I'm sorry."

She met his eyes in the glass. "About what?"

"Knocking you down. Doing that." He tilted his chin toward the cut.

"Yeah, I'd much rather have been shot."

He couldn't argue with her logic, but he still felt guilty. Despite the situation, he should have thought of some other method of putting her out of harm's way.

"Actually, I don't think I said thank-you for saving me from my own stupidity." She turned to face him, the Band-Aid now in place. "I mean that," she added, when he didn't respond. "I never dreamed any of them would fire on me."

"I think he panicked." Jake couldn't figure out why he was defending the bastard. Other than the distress he saw in her eyes.

"Of course, I also never thought *any* of this could happen in Waverly," she added.

"The kidnapping?"

"That. The mob scene at the station. This, out here to-night." She shook her head. "It's not what we're like. Not what the people here are like."

"You aren't responsible for their actions."

"No. Only for my own." The upward tilt of her lips was a little tremulous. "Which means I need to get out to Lincoln Greene's like I told Dean I would."

"You want me to go with you?"

The sound she made was part laughter, part derision. "Despite my earlier ineptitude, I think I can manage to get myself over there in one piece."

His inclination was to argue with her, but he had sense

enough to realize her ego had already taken a major hit to-night. Seeming to doubt her competence would be another.

"Then I'll walk you to your car."

"You think he's still out there?" She sounded surprised.

He didn't. Despite that conviction, however, Jake found himself wishing that the bastard might be. Especially when he considered the square of plastic covering Eden's temple and the fair, bloodstained hair that fell over it.

If not tonight, I hope to God that one day I get another chance at that coward.

Chapter Seven

"All I know is what I told you. It was in the carport when I went to bed. Laurie's told you the same thing."

"You hear anything after you turned in?" Dean asked.

Lincoln Greene ran a hand through his thinning hair. "I told you that, too. Carport's on the other side of the house from the bedroom. You couldn't hear a bomb if it went off out there. Not from our room."

"Link wouldn't hear a bomb go off if it was *in* the bedroom," Greene's wife said. "Not as sound as *he* sleeps."

"You didn't hear anything either, Laurie?" Eden asked.

As angry as Lincoln had been earlier, she believed he might have done something stupid like going out to Jake's place. She didn't believe, however, that his wife would connive with him to cover it up if he had. Laurie Greene was front row center at every service of the Pentecostal church and highly respected in the community.

"I heard Link snoring from about nine on. I promise you, he didn't go anywhere. If his truck ended up out at the Wells' place tonight, somebody else drove it."

"That's what I've been trying to tell you," Lincoln said. "You know me better than that, Dean. I'm not gonna go out there and do something stupid. I'll speak my piece, but whatever happens with Underwood, that's up to the law. I'm no hothead."

"You seemed pretty hot this afternoon," Dean said mildly.

"Yeah, well, everybody was worked up. Just the thought of some pervert doing something to that little girl..." Greene's lips tightened, but he didn't finish the sentence.

"Was the truck locked?" Eden asked into the silence that had fallen, as, unwillingly, they were all forced to remember what this was really about.

Greene laughed. "Parked in my driveway? Never saw any need. Not around here."

"It might be a good idea from now on," Dean cautioned.

"Will y'all give me a ride out there, so I can bring my truck home?"

"I think the last thing you want to do tonight is to set foot on Mr. Underwood's property," Eden said. "Let's just say he wouldn't be welcoming visitors right now."

"Then how am I gonna get my truck? I got to have a way to get to the store in the morning."

"You get Laurie to take you in," Dean suggested.

"I don't see why we should be inconvenienced—"

"Whoever was driving that truck tonight took a shot at me," Eden said. "That makes the vehicle part of a crime scene. We'll return it to you as soon as the department has had a chance to check for prints and anything else that might tell us who drove it out there."

"And how long will that take?" Lincoln's tone was almost as belligerent as it had been this afternoon.

"It'll take as long as it takes. That'll be up to the chief." Dean's words were clearly a warning. One Greene was smart enough to heed.

"You all call me when you're done with it. All right?"

"Of course," Eden said. "By the way, anybody but you and Laurie ever drive the truck?"

Greene looked at his wife, who shrugged. "Laurie won't drive the thing. Too rough riding for her. If you're looking for prints, you'll find plenty of mine, but..." He shook his head.

I don't guess anybody but me's been behind the wheel since bought it from Steiner's over in Moss Point. They might can ell you the name of the previous owner."

"You come on down in the morning and let us take your rints," Dean suggested. "Maybe on your way to the store."

"You want to fingerprint me?"

"Just so we can see who else's are on the wheel," Dean ssured.

"And what if nobody else's are? What if they wore gloves r something? Y'all gonna come back at me about this?"

"We're going to take a good look at everything," Eden said. "And when we have, you'll get your truck back. Laurie." She odded at Greene's wife. "Y'all get some sleep. We'll see you a the morning."

As soon as the front door closed behind the Greenes, Dean sked, "You want me to send somebody out to the Wells' lace to pick up that truck?"

"And get 'em killed?" Eden asked. "Underwood was out alking whoever had pulled Lincoln's truck onto his road hen I got there. My impression was that it wouldn't much ave mattered to him if they'd been wearing a uniform."

"Is that how you got that cut on your head?" Dean asked s he climbed into the driver's seat of the cruiser.

"This?" As Eden settled into the passenger seat, she raised er hand to touch the gash she'd forgotten and winced at the esulting pain. "I got this being naive enough to think I knew hat everyone in this town was and wasn't capable of."

"What does that mean?"

She was aware that, in the dimness of the interior, Dean ad taken his eyes off the road to look at her. "It means I alled out to whoever drove that truck out there. Asked them o come out and talk."

"That's when they took a shot at you."

"Two, actually. Underwood knocked me down after the

first. Maybe saved my life. I hit my head on something a
I fell." She touched the place again and then deliberatel
lowered her hand.

It reminded her of what might have been. She had literal
felt the bullet go by. Whoever fired it hadn't been trying
frighten her.

"You need to get that looked at?" Dean asked.

"It's fine."

"I can do this on my own, Chief."

"I know. I just think it might go better if I'm with you."

They didn't talk again during the fifteen minutes or so
took to reach the turnoff, each lost in his or her own thought
And too many of hers revolved around the man who'd rescue
her from her own naïveté.

"Hit the light bar," she ordered, as they turned down th
road leading to the Wells' home place. "Let him know wh
we are."

Dean obeyed, the flashing strobes adding a touch of su
realism to the festoons of moss that decorated the trees. A
they approached the rear of the vehicle they'd come to in
pound, Jake Underwood stepped out of the shadows in fro
of them, the rifle he'd carried earlier still expertly cradled
his hands.

Dean slammed on the brakes, stopping the car with on
inches to spare. The tall, militarily erect figure before the
didn't waver, despite that near miss.

"Sweet Jesus," Dean breathed.

More a prayer than a profanity, Eden decided, amuse
despite herself. She opened the door and stepped out.

"I'm going to send somebody out to pick that up," sh
indicated the truck behind him, "and take it into town."

"You might want to take a look at what's in the bed." Jak
still hadn't moved.

The words, or perhaps the tone in which they'd bee

poken, chilled her. A dozen possible scenarios involving "what's in the bed" raced through her mind.

Not Raine, she prayed, rejecting the worst of them. *Dear God, don't let it be Raine.*

If there was a child in the car—even a child's body, she ealized belatedly—Jake Underwood would never have told er to take a look. That kind of sadistic behavior didn't fit the haracterization of the man that was building in her head.

She walked toward the truck, reaching for the latch of the ailgate. Dean's command stopped her.

"Don't touch anything until we've had a chance to print t."

"You can see it from here." Jake moved beside her, shining he flashlight she hadn't been aware he carried into the bed.

It took a moment to identify what she was looking at. ome kind of wadded-up fabric. Her brain registered details utomatically, even as she attempted to make sense of why ake had thought this was important.

Tiny pink-and-white checks, like a child's sundress. Except t wasn't a dress. It was…

A gingham quilt, she realized. In the glare of the light Jake eld, the stitches that crisscrossed the material were discern-ble.

"I didn't remember this from any of the news stories," Jake aid. "I thought maybe it was something your department was vithholding from the public. Something to help discriminate etween someone who has real information…"

The sentence trailed as Eden stepped away from the truck. he swallowed the bile that had climbed into her throat. On ome level she was aware that Dean had moved around her o peer into the bed.

"What the hell?" he breathed softly.

"I thought maybe that belonged to the Nolan girl." Jake's oice had lost its certainty.

"Not that we're aware of. Did Margo mention a blanke like that to you, Chief?"

Eden shook her head, fighting the urge to shiver, despit the humid blanket of Gulf Coast heat that surrounded them "It's a quilt."

"Quilt. Whatever. Did the Nolans mention something lik that was missing?"

Eden knew the silence following her deputy chief's ques tion stretched too long, but she couldn't seem to formula an answer that made sense. None of this made sense.

You're being ridiculous. Snap out of it and start actin like the person who's in charge of finding a missing child. child who went missing four days ago.

"They never indicated that any kind of bedding was taken she managed.

She forced her gaze up and found that, although Dean w. still focused on the quilt, Jake was watching her. She opene her mouth, trying to pull in enough of the thick air to figh the light-headedness that threatened to take her down.

"We'll bag it and take it over to Margo in the morning. Se if she can identify it," Dean said. "In the confusion, mayb they didn't even realize it was gone."

Eden nodded, still aware of the intensity of Jake's scrutin This time—thankfully—he didn't ask if she was all righ Nor did he mouth any of the platitudes people usually us to someone who appears on the verge of fainting. The gra eyes simply held on her face, as if offering a strength sh desperately needed.

"Eden?" Dean asked, pulling her gaze back to hin "What's the matter? You look like you've seen a ghost."

Maybe she had. The now-ghostly memory of another litt girl who had gone missing more than twenty years ago. Take from her bed. Taken from the same room where her sist slept.

The kidnapper of that child had wrapped her in

pink-and-white gingham quilt. One her grandmother had made for her by hand.

And then no one had ever seen her again.

Chapter Eight

"Are you sure, Margo? Kids have so much stuff these days. Maybe it was something somebody gave her..." Eden knew she was pressing too hard, but she had tried to convince herself through most of the night that this had nothing to do with her sister's disappearance. The surest way to do that would be to connect the quilt to the Nolans.

"I don't remember ever seeing that before. Raine's favorite color is purple. Everything we bought the past few years has been some shade of that. You want me to ask Storm? She's the one who likes pink."

Other than the brief questioning the MBI had insisted on, Eden had tried to protect the Nolans' other daughter from any kind of interrogation. Perhaps Storm was a witness to what had happened that night, but the child had insisted to the agents that she'd been asleep when her sister was taken.

"I don't want to cause her any more distress than she's already endured," Eden said.

"Either she recognizes this or not. If she does..." Margo's voice broke. "If she does," she began again, "we need to know. If she doesn't, and I don't think she will, then there's not gonna be any kind of emotional reaction to it. Right?"

Eden hesitated, remembering the hours of interrogation the police in Ohio had put her through. Asking the same thing over and over again. As if they believed that, if she only tried a little harder, she might suddenly think of something that would help find her sister.

But Margo was right. They needed to know. And if Storm was the best source for this information...

"I think you're probably right," she conceded.

"Then I'll go get her." Margo rose, handing Eden the quilt on her way out of the room.

Slightly soiled from the bed of Lincoln Greene's truck, the fabric had been carefully bagged by the department's evidence technician. As Eden placed it across her knees, her eyes fell to the stitches.

They were small and far too regular to be handmade, even by a quilter as skilled as her grandmother. The technician had verified her impression that this was not only machine-made, but relatively new. The eerie similarity to the one her grandmother had sewn so long ago was apparently a bizarre coincidence.

"You go on now," Margo said from the doorway. She urged her daughter forward with her hands on her shoulders. "The chief wants to see if you recognize what's in the bag."

The little girl walked forward until she was standing at Eden's knee. She smelled of sunshine and baby shampoo, the sweet, clean fragrances of childhood.

"What is it?"

"It's a quilt. I just wondered if it belonged to you or to Raine."

The blond head moved side to side, but the blue eyes didn't lift from the bag. "It's dirty."

"I know. You think Raine had a quilt like this?"

"Raine doesn't like pink all that much. Everybody knows that."

"I didn't. Maybe somebody else who didn't know gave this to her."

The child raised her eyes, seeming surprised by Eden's

comment. "She likes lavender best. Only sometimes, she calls it lilac. Like the flower."

"And you've never seen this before."

"We don't have dirty stuff. Do we, Mama?"

"Look at it, Storm. It's important. You ever seen that before?"

"No, ma'am."

"You sure?"

"Yes, ma'am."

"Okay." Margo's eyes met Eden's, her brows raised in question.

Eden nodded.

"You go on back upstairs and play," Margo directed. "I'll be up in a minute."

"Maybe he gave it to her." The little girl's comment had been directed to Eden rather than her mother.

"He?" she asked softly.

"Whoever took her. Maybe he gave it to her to make her feel safe."

"Safe?" Margo's question was full of the same horror Eden felt. "What in the world do you mean, Storm?"

"Like a lovey. Something for her to hold on to. Maybe he gave it to her so she wouldn't be afraid of having to sleep away from home."

WHEN EDEN GOT back to the station, she found Dean had also returned. She tossed the bagged quilt onto her desk and then poured a cup of coffee from the pot that was always kept full.

"The Nolans recognize it?"

"Margo said it wasn't theirs. She suggested the sister look at it. Storm said she'd never seen it before. Then she said…" For some reason Eden's throat tightened, but she forced the words out. "She said maybe the kidnapper gave it to Raine to make her feel safe when she had to sleep away from home." She raised her gaze to watch the impact of that on her deputy.

"Good Lord almighty. Where'd she get that idea?"

"I don't know. Maybe just because we were asking if it belonged to Raine. I guess I need to tell the agents what she said. What'd the Greenes say about it?"

"No quilt in the truck. Never has been. Lincoln was sure it wasn't there when he parked it last night. He stopped to pick up some stuff at Winn-Dixie, and he put the groceries in the bed. Said he would have noticed something like that if it had been there then."

Eden nodded, her eyes on the evidence bag. "What do you think?"

"May not have a thing to do with the kidnapping. May just belong to whoever took the truck."

"Why bring it along?"

"Hell, Eden, I don't know. None of this makes sense. Why did they go out to Underwood's in the first place? Why did they take a shot at you? It's all crazy."

"They find any prints in the truck?"

"Wiped clean as a whistle. Steering wheel. Dash. Door handles."

"That ought to make Lincoln feel better."

"How so?"

"He wouldn't take the trouble to wipe down his own truck and then leave it out there. That makes no sense, either."

Winton stuck his head into her opened door. "Major Underwood's out front. He wants to see you."

Eden met Dean's eyes. He shrugged and began to rise from the chair he'd been sprawled in when she'd arrived.

"Stay," she told him. And then to Winton, "He say what he wants to see me about?"

"Nope. Want me to ask?"

"Not really. Send him on back."

"Maybe he's here to file a complaint against the trespasser last night," Dean said, when the younger deputy disappeared. "Make it official."

"Of course."

Eden was relieved to have such a logical explanation. One she should have thought of herself. Instead, the only thing that had come to mind when Winton said Jake wanted to see her was that he'd had another flashback.

In her more rational moments, she was able to dismiss those as the result of whatever injury Jake had suffered, combined with the incessant media coverage of the kidnapping. As the search had grown more desperate and the pressure had built, however, Jake Underwood's "visions" had become almost the only thing standing between her and total despair.

The thought that he might come to tell her that Raine Nolan was no longer haunting his flashbacks was something she'd been dreading almost as much as someone calling to say they'd found the child's body. *Almost* as much.

"He's moved her."

Eden looked up to find Jake standing in the door to her office. His shoulders filled the frame, the muscles of his chest stretching the navy T-shirt he wore. She had time to acknowledge both before his words registered.

"*Moved* her?"

"She isn't in the dugout anymore." He shook his head, the movement clearly indicating puzzlement. "I don't know how to describe where she is. It's still dark. Damp. But it doesn't appear to be underground. Or at least not *in* the ground."

"You had another flashback."

Jake's eyes briefly considered Dean, but he didn't respond to his stating the obvious. He looked back at Eden instead.

"Maybe concrete. It didn't last long enough for me to be certain. That's nothing more than an impression, but I know the roots weren't there. And it wasn't dirt."

"Okay. Anything else?" Despite the surge of relief she'd felt at Jake's description, Eden worked at keeping her responses neutral. Dean didn't place any faith in what Underwood claimed to see. And as far as he knew, neither did she.

"She didn't seem as scared."

"Because he'd moved her?" Dean asked. "You think she was more afraid of the other place?"

"I don't know. All I know is the level of fear didn't seem as strong."

"That's good to hear. Thanks for coming to tell us." Too patronizing, Eden realized belatedly. As if she was making fun of what he'd just said.

When Jake looked back at her, there was a furrow between his dark brows. "You *asked* me to let you know."

She had. She just hadn't admitted to Dean that she'd done that.

"Was this…" she hesitated, knowing she needed to choose her words carefully. "The flashback. Was that last night or this morning?"

"Sometime before dawn."

"You sure you weren't dreaming?" Dean asked.

"I didn't get all that much sleep last night."

The image of Jake appearing before them out of the darkness, that rifle cradled in his hands, was suddenly in Eden's head. He'd probably kept watch at his place all night.

On patrol. Like the soldier he'd once been.

She realized then that she had gone off the deep end with this. Giving credence to the visions of a man who'd been physically and emotionally damaged by his experiences in combat.

Maybe the townspeople were right. Maybe Jake had passed that lie-detector test because he was no longer able to distinguish between fantasy and reality.

Making sure this investigation did exactly that was her job. Not chasing ghosts from Jake Underwood's past.

Or from her own.

"We're setting up new grids for our teams this morning," she said, to ease the tension that seemed to have sprung up between the three of them. "We're also going to re-cover some of the territory that we searched during the first twenty-four hours. The possibility existed from the beginning that Raine would be moved. Maybe he's taken her to a place he thinks is safe because it's already been searched."

"I'd like to help," Jake said. "Something may seem famil-iar."

Because he'd seen it in his flashback. Could this conversa-tion become any more insane?

"Given what happened last night," Dean said, "I don't think that's a good idea. Folks were pretty riled up when they heard what you're claiming."

Again Jake looked at the older man. *"Claiming?"*

"The only people who believe in visions around here are the Pentecostals. And they don't see dead children in theirs."

"Dean," Eden warned.

"Missing children," he amended. "No matter what *we* believe about what you've told us—or about you, for that matter—it's what the people who were out at your place last night believe that you need to be worried about."

Although Eden could see only Jake's profile, she was aware of the slow upward lift at the corner of his mouth.

"I think I can manage to deal with them *and* help with the search. Chief Reddick?" His eyes returned to her, clearly waiting for permission.

"I know you want to help. And I commend you for that. Frankly, I don't have the officers to spearhead the search teams *and* protect you. You'd be taking away resources that can be better utilized elsewhere."

"I'm not asking for protection." There was amusement in his voice this time.

"No, but if the anger directed at you that was expressed to this department yesterday flares up again, I'll have to pro-vide it. To you. *Or* to whoever believes they need to take some action because they think you had something to do with Raine's disappearance."

The silence lasted long enough to be uncomfortable. When Jake finally broke it, his voice was controlled, but no longer amused. "I don't want to make your job harder. Good luck with your search."

He nodded to Dean before he went back through the doorway. They listened again to his limping footsteps down the tiled hallway and then to Winton's goodbye.

When the outer door closed behind him, Dean laughed. "You had me going there for a minute, Chief."

"About what?"

"Thinking you were taking all that vision stuff seriously."

"Flashbacks."

"Does it matter?"

She shook her head, which despite the coffee had begun to ache. Too little sleep and too much anxiety. And either could lead her to make the kind of misjudgment that would cost Raine Nolan her life.

If she is still alive, she silently amended. And the reality was that was becoming less likely by the second.

Chapter Nine

Jake didn't know what had changed with Eden since last night, but if he were a betting man, he'd have put money on that sarcastic deputy having something to do with it. This certainly wasn't the first time he'd made a fool of himself by taking a woman at her word, but he swore it would be the last time he'd open himself up to ridicule by the Waverly Police Department. And that included their chief.

Still seething, he had almost reached his truck when he became aware he was being followed down the main drag of town. Such a loss of focus might in other circumstances have cost him his life. Here it meant only that the confrontation that was to occur wouldn't take place on his terms.

He opened the door to his truck, more than willing to get in it and leave. Considering all that had happened in the past twenty-four hours, he didn't expect that he would be allowed to do that. He was right.

"Seen any more little girls in your dreams, Major?"

The voice was strongly Southern. Not the educated Southern the deputy spoke or the quasi-Southern of the chief. This was the backwater dialect that owed its twang to both African and Cajun influences.

Jake ignored the comment, putting his left foot on the wide running board in preparation for climbing up into the high seat. Before he could do that, someone grabbed a handful of his shirt and pulled.

With most of his weight on his bad leg, it buckled, throwing him backward and onto his assailant. They both went down, but the other man jumped quickly to his feet. Before Jake could get his good leg under him, the toe of his opponent's boot caught him under the chin.

If his reflexes had been a fraction slower, the blow would probably have knocked him out. Instead, he managed to jerk his head and torso to the side, avoiding the brunt of the kick.

His defensive move pitched his upper body back onto his elbows and forearms. Relatively stabilized, he raised both feet and caught the redneck's still uplifted leg between them. Twisting his lower body to the right, he threw his assailant, off-balanced by the kick, to the ground.

The side of the bastard's head struck the curb with a thud. Before he could rise, Jake was on him. His right arm suffered from the same weakness that affected his leg, but he'd always had a good left cross. He used it now. This time it was the back of the man's skull that made contact with the pavement, but the hollow sound when it struck was the same.

Before Jake could follow up with a second blow, several sets of hands grabbed his upper arms, pulling him backward and to his feet. Once they had him upright, they didn't let go.

He struggled to free himself, using the tricks of a trade he'd practiced for almost twenty years. Even as he felt one pair of hands lose their grip, however, others replaced them. Engaged in employing elbows and feet and even his head against the men who held him, he watched as the one he'd downed pushed himself to his feet.

His attacker looked at the blood he had wiped from his mouth, and then, using that same hand, drove his fist into Jake's face with every ounce of strength in his body. And held from behind, there wasn't a hell of a lot Jake could do to avoid the blow.

The scene around him blackened as he fought to retain consciousness. With a mob like this, he knew that if he went down, they would finish him off with their feet.

They might not set out to kill him, but they could. Despite the brutal beatings portrayed in movies, where the hero gets up and walks away without a bruise or a broken bone, the reality of that kind of pummeling was usually very different.

As his initial attacker followed up with a left to his stomach, Jake allowed his body to sag back against the men who were holding him. That movement allowed him to go with the direction of the punch rather than absorb its full force. It also caused them to tighten their grip on his arms in order to hold him erect.

Once they had secured their hold, Jake swung his left leg up, the toe of his boot catching his attacker at the most vulnerable place on his body. As the man screamed and doubled over in agony, Jake twisted free from the stunned group behind him.

He pushed the keening man back with his left arm before he spun to face the crowd. Knees bent, legs slightly apart for balance, he prepared for the next redneck who wanted a piece of him.

None of the men who had come to the aid of his assailant looked eager to take his place. And since he was still making that same high-pitched keening sound, Jake began to straighten, preparing to get into his truck.

Eden's voice stopped him. "That's enough," she ordered. "What the hell are you doing?"

For a moment Jake thought the question had been directed at him. Only when the men between them began to part to make way for their chief of police did he understand she was talking to the crowd.

"What's wrong with you? Have you lost every shred of common sense and decency you ever possessed?"

By that time she was standing in front of him. Her

cornflower-blue eyes widened when she saw his face. Her mouth opened and then closed with a snap. She turned to the crowd. "Get out of here. Now. And take him with you."

With her head she indicated the man Jake had kicked. The noise he'd been making had softened into a series of moans.

"I'm ashamed of y'all," Eden said. "This isn't the way we handle things in this town."

"He knows more than he's tellin' you," someone accused.

"Major Underwood was wounded in the service of our country." There was a mutter of disapproval or derision, but Eden continued to speak over it. "*And* he passed a lie-detector test given by the FBI. We have *no* reason to believe he is in any way connected with Raine Nolan's disappearance."

"Except he claims he knows where she is. That he's seen her. Something's not right about that, Chief."

Jake couldn't tell who had spoken, but there was a chorus of agreement.

"Major Underwood suffers from flashbacks. Perhaps because the kidnapping has been on all our minds—" Once more Eden was interrupted by jeers. When she began again, her voice was stronger, filled with emotion. "We go to bed at night and get up in the morning besieged by the media coverage of this kidnapping. I dream about that little girl every night, and I'd be willing to bet I'm not the only one here who's done that. She's on all our hearts and minds. If you can't understand how someone—" She stopped, as if suddenly seeming to realize the direction her argument had taken.

There were no catcalls from the crowd that had at some point during her impassioned speech grown quiet. In that unexpected silence, Eden looked at him.

Jake didn't wait to hear whatever else she intended to say. He turned instead and limped toward his truck. Gritting his teeth, he pulled himself into the driver's seat and then slammed the door. Nobody tried to stop him as he turned the key and put the vehicle into gear.

Why *would* they interfere? he mocked himself. After all, their chief of police had explained the whole thing to them. Just some crazy-ass ex-soldier, so brain-damaged that the voices in his television made him think he could see that little girl.

Don't attack him, she'd urged them. Pity the poor screwed-up bastard instead.

Just like she did.

WHEN HE GOT home, he discovered his injuries were less extensive than he'd expected. After a hot shower and a couple of the pain pills from the prescription the Army docs had given him, he began to feel almost human again.

Part of that was because he felt he'd acquitted himself fairly well, given the odds. The sense of satisfaction he'd gotten from listening to that mouth-breather scream had gone a long way toward soothing his injured pride, even if it hadn't done much for his bruised ribs or swollen jaw.

It hadn't been the fight that had driven him to take his battered body out to his grandmother's woodpile, however. The ax he'd bought to replace the one he'd found rusting in the stump where his grandfather had once split logs felt satisfyingly right in his hands. As did the sound the wood made when the blade hit solidly.

Intent on what he was doing, he didn't hear the police cruiser pull up in front. Only when he stopped to wipe sweat out of his eyes did he become aware that Eden was standing in the side yard watching him.

"Don't you have anything else to do?" he asked, before he turned his attention to the next piece of oak.

"One of the search teams found bones out at the old McCoy place."

Jake's heart stopped. He lowered the ax, turning to look at her.

He had believed he would know. That his connection to Raine was strong enough that he'd be aware if she were no longer alive. Apparently he'd been wrong.

"They belonged to a calf," Eden went on, her voice emotionless. "Or a big dog. Not human anyway. I'm on my way back to the station to file a report."

"And you just couldn't resist coming by here to say hello." He raised the ax again, bringing it down hard enough to cleave the log with one blow.

"Can we talk?"

"I thought that's what we were doing." He refused to look at her.

"Then could you please stop doing that?"

"Why?" He placed the next log on the stump, taking his time to position it.

"I'm sorry."

He raised the ax to the full reach of his arms and then brought it down on the wood. The result wasn't as dramatic as the last had been, but at least it gave him something to do other than remember what he'd felt standing out on that street this morning. Exposed for what he was to every yokel in town.

"I needed to calm them down," Eden went on. "I didn't think… I thought that was something they could all relate to."

"Being crazy? Good plan."

"That isn't what I said."

"Well, that's what they heard."

"That's what *you* heard. It wasn't what I meant."

He lowered the ax, finally turning to look at her. The shadows under her eyes were like bruises, her face almost gaunt. The sun-touched hair had been slicked back into a ponytail.

Paradoxically, the style made her appear younger, despite the physical toll the kidnapping had clearly taken.

"What *did* you mean?"

"I've lived with this for four days. I think about her every waking minute. And it seems like half of the other minutes, too. She's inside my head when I'm awake and when I sleep. It's all-consuming. I meant to suggest this morning that hearing about the kidnapping endlessly is bound to…" She stopped, shaking her head.

"I didn't know who Raine Nolan was when I had that first flashback."

She took a breath, deep enough that it lifted her shoulders. Her breasts moved under the uniform shirt, forcing Jake to turn back to the stump and the waiting log.

"I had to tell them *something*."

"Yeah? Well, tell *me* something. Have you just been humoring me all along? Pretending to believe that there might be something to what I'm seeing and then dismissing it during the actual investigation." The memory of her chief deputy's disdain was another humiliation.

"Maybe. At first. But I went out to the caves, remember. And I told the search-team leaders to alert everybody to the possibility that the kidnapper might have constructed an in-ground bunker to hide her."

"Not exactly a novel concept."

"No," she admitted. "There are certainly precedents for that."

"But deep down inside, you didn't really believe that what I saw had anything to do with that child's abduction?"

She hesitated, seeming to think about her answer. Maybe trying for honesty.

"I don't know," she said finally.

"You tell anybody?"

"What you said?" She shook her head.

"So how did everybody in town come to know about it?"

"If you didn't mention it—"

"Do I strike you as stupid enough to go around spreading the word that I'd seen that little girl in a flashback?"

"Then obviously someone in the department leaked the information. That's one of the things I wanted to talk to you about. I know you're resistant to the suggestion, but I'd like to put an officer out here. Maybe just at night—"

"I thought your resources were spread too thin to guard me." He made no effort to hide his sarcasm.

"They were. They are. But after what happened today—"

"No."

"What?"

"I said no. I don't want anybody out here at night. Or in the day. Whatever manpower you've got needs to be used to find that kid."

He raised the ax again, sighting on the wood before he struck, successfully splitting this one into two pieces. He bent to pick them up and tossed them onto the growing pile.

"You think she's still alive?"

He took a second to school his features before he looked up, but despite his attempt at control, fury bubbled dangerously near the surface. *Screw her.* She had ridiculed what he had told her in front of an audience of hillbillies out for his blood, and now she was looking for reassurance that she still had a hope in hell of finding that little girl before—

He swallowed his rage at the reminder of what this was really about. The reason he'd been willing to risk exactly what had happened this morning.

"For what it's worth…yeah, I think she's still alive."

Another deep breath, again lifting her breasts. This time he deliberately allowed his gaze to focus on the movement. When he met her eyes again, a flush of color stained her cheeks.

"Thank you."

She sounded as if she meant it, but he was too angry to

care anymore. "Don't thank me, lady. Just do your damn job for a change and find that kid."

If he had expected her to react with outrage to that unfair accusation, he was disappointed. Maybe the flush on her cheeks deepened, but she didn't dispute what he'd said. She nodded instead and then turned to walk back to the patrol car, her head down.

Bothered by the dejection in the set of her narrow shoulders, Jake went back to the stacked logs to select his next victim. It had been a hell of a lot easier to hang on to his anger before she'd asked that final question.

He had told her what she wanted to hear because it was the truth. And he no longer gave a tinker's damn what she did with the information, he told himself, as he positioned the wood on the stump.

She could make it into the punch line of jokes in her department. Or broadcast it to the vultures in town who wanted his blood. Or tell it to the scavengers who made their living reporting on the sufferings of victims like the Nolans.

All he knew was what he had seen this morning. And that if anybody was going to locate that little girl based on the connection he had to her, it was going to have to be him.

Chapter Ten

Eden had put off calling the office until she was turning into her own drive. If there had been any new developments while she was out on this latest wild-goose chase, she wasn't sure she wanted to hear about them. Because, based on the brief meeting she'd had this afternoon with the special agents from Jackson, at this point in the investigation she shouldn't expect anything but bad news.

"What's going on?" she asked when her chief deputy answered.

They had begun using their cell phones for conversations like this after the leak about Underwood's flashbacks. Not only did that method insure that what they said wouldn't be spread all over town, it allowed them the freedom to do something they both needed to do—to be completely honest about the investigation and about what they were feeling.

"Nothing. Where are you?" Dean sounded distracted, but then, he'd been dealing with the media most of the day. Even the street fight this morning had made the five-o'clock news.

"In my driveway. If I don't get some sleep, I'm going to be a liability to everybody else on the highway."

"Don't set an alarm."

She laughed. "I haven't needed one since this started."

Between department business, the media and townspeople who felt perfectly free to dial her home number for updates, she had been awakened every day by the phone. On the nights she'd managed to sleep at all.

"So the idiots out at the McCoys' couldn't tell the difference between a cow and a little girl."

She blocked that unwanted image from her mind. Something she'd had a lot of practice with lately. "It wasn't as easy as you'd think."

"You all right? You sound…"

Dean's pause could have been filled with any number of appropriate adjectives. *Exhausted. Discouraged.* As low as she could remember feeling since her mother's death. All of them applied.

"I'm okay," she lied. "I stopped by on the way home to apologize to Underwood."

Another pause. This one longer than the last.

"You felt that was necessary?"

"It was to me. No matter what we believe about the flashbacks, he came to us in a genuine attempt to help. Somebody in the department leaked what he told us, putting him in danger. And then I publicly humiliated him today."

"Underwood's a big boy, Eden. And he's got to know he's got problems. You tell him that he needs to come in tomorrow and press charges?"

"Sorry. I didn't think about it. I was so relieved when Dr. Murphy said that what they'd found wasn't a child—"

"I understand," Dean interrupted. "But Underwood needs to know that we can't hold Porter longer than forty-eight hours if he doesn't fill out the paperwork."

Dave Porter, the man who had pulled Jake out of his truck and thrown the first punch, was the only one they'd arrested, and the charge had been disorderly conduct and causing a public disturbance. They'd done that in an attempt to warn anybody else who might think attacking the major was a good idea. If Jake pressed assault charges, it might create a

tronger deterrent and solve a problem the department didn't
need right now.

"You want to call him?" Dean asked. "Or you want me
to?"

"It might be better coming from you. I'm definitely not his
favorite person right now. He might refuse to come in, just
because I asked. You staying at the office a while?"

"Yeah. You get some sleep."

"Special Agent Franklin was out at the McCoys'."

"Anything new?"

"They're convinced she's dead. They're going back to
Jackson tomorrow. That's not for public consumption, by
the way."

"Can't say I blame them. You gonna tell the Nolans?"

"Eventually." Just not tonight.

"Want me to do it?"

"Thanks, but that kind of thing is really my job."

Another pause. She wondered if Dean was thinking what
she was. That, as Jake Underwood had reminded her, finding
Raine had also been *her* job. One she had failed at miserably.

"See you tomorrow, then."

"Don't stay too late," she urged. "We're all running on
fumes. And I don't think anything else will happen tonight.
At least nothing that can't wait until tomorrow."

Unless that next set of bones does belong to a child.

She closed her cell and climbed out of the patrol car. Every
part of her body ached. Too little sleep. Too little food. Too
few results.

She turned her key in the lock and welcomed the artificially cooled air that rushed out to greet her. The house was
dark, but in its welcome familiarity, she didn't bother to turn
on the lights.

She headed toward the back instead, removing her utility
belt to drape over the back of the couch. She walked down
the hall to the bathroom, unbuttoning her shirt as she did. She

pulled it out of her pants and then off over her head befor
she put the stopper in the tub and turned on the hot water
She let it run as she removed the rest of her clothing.

She wasn't sure she could keep her eyes open long enoug
to soak out the bone-deep fatigue, but she was going to try
And she needed to eat something before she lay down. Bath
food, bed.

Wearing only her panties and bra, she walked across th
hall to her bedroom—cool, dark and too inviting—to get
clean nightgown. Resisting temptation, she didn't even loo
in the direction of the bed as she retrieved the gown from he
drawer and started back toward the hall.

Something she couldn't quite put her finger on nagged a
her, however, causing her to stop at the doorway and the
turn to survey the room. Her bed was unmade, as it had bee
during the past few hectic days.

It didn't seem to be in quite the same condition she'd le
it in this morning. The covers were too neatly turned back o
the far side, with both pillows positioned against the head
board. Since she cradled one of those as she slept, it usuall
ended up aligned vertically along the center of the wide ma
tress in the morning. She would have sworn it had been the
today.

She took a step forward, trying to remember if she ha
straightened the bed when she'd crawled out of it. Was it pos
sible she was so sleep deprived she had no memory of doin
that?

Another step carried her near enough to realize somethir
lay partially concealed by the arrangement of the bedding. .
bulge that began in the center of one of those precisely place
pillows.

Hands trembling, she reached out and flicked on the bec
side lamp. Even with the object in the bed illuminated, it too
a second for her brain to process what she was seeing.

Not a child, which had been her first terrifying though

And nothing that had ever been animate, despite the deliberate attempt to make it appear lifelike.

It was a doll. A baby doll—almost life-size—its rounded plastic head centered on her pillow.

Having made that identification, Eden still didn't move, her hand frozen on the switch of the lamp as she came to a series of undeniable conclusions. While she'd been at work, someone had placed a doll in her bed and covered it as you would tuck in a child for the night.

Her heart began to pound. She gagged, thankful that her stomach was empty. She put a shaking hand over her mouth, unable to prevent the tears that flooded her eyes.

Her instinct was to flee. Get her clothes and just get out. Except this was her home. Her sanctuary. The thought that someone had invaded it to do this vileness…

Forcing herself to move, she took the three steps that would carry her to the closet and ripped her robe off its hanger. As she struggled into the garment, she ran toward the kitchen and the back door.

It was locked, the dead bolt shot, just as it had been when she'd checked it last night. She turned to retrace her steps to secure the front door, trying each of the windows as she passed by them.

Two lifted when she pushed against their sashes, but they were the ones she occasionally raised to air out the house. She couldn't swear they'd been locked after the last time she'd done that.

She could find nothing else suspicious. Nothing had been disturbed. There was nothing missing and nothing out of place.

Only the doll, carefully placed in her bed. And positioned exactly as the other one had been.

Knowing the bath she'd anticipated would no longer be in the least relaxing, she walked back to turn off the water. She stood a moment, watching the steam rise off its surface, trying to think what she should do. Before she had decided whether to call Dean and get someone out here to do the kind of examination of the premises they'd do for any other break-in, the doorbell rang.

Although it wasn't late, it *was* after dark. People usually wouldn't come to the door without calling first, unless...

Unless it was an emergency. Or bad news.

She took a deep breath, trying to prepare for something she'd been dreading since the morning Raine disappeared. And realized she would never be prepared for what she feared she was about to hear.

She pulled the front on her robe together as she walked to the living room. Her utility belt was still lying over the back of the couch. Given that she had no way of knowing who was waiting on her stoop, she slipped her weapon out of it, concealing the Glock in the folds of her robe.

"Who is it?" she asked, as she turned on the porch light.

"Jake Underwood."

The last person she might have expected to show up at her front door unannounced. Considering how angry he'd been this afternoon, she couldn't think of a reason why he might have come.

All the doubts she'd originally had about his motives the morning he'd showed up in the office with his flashback story flooded her head. Those had long since been pushed aside by the trust that had grown between them. What if she'd been wrong? What if he'd been the person who'd broken into her house?

Except that made no sense. How could Jake have known anything about the doll?

"What do you want?"

"To apologize."

Which was even more unexpected than his showing up here without warning. As she was trying to decide whether or not to believe him, he spoke again.

"I can do that from out here, if you want."

Did she really believe he intended to do her harm? And if ot, why would she hesitate to let him in?

After all, she'd gone out to *his* place to apologize. Why vouldn't he think it was okay for him to do the same?

She undid the chain, turned the locks and opened the door. he swelling on his face looked even worse under the glare of he porch's yellow bug-repellant light. And for the first time ince she'd known him, he looked uncertain.

"Come in." She stepped back, giving him room to enter.

Although he'd been dressed in his usual faded jeans and -shirt this afternoon, tonight he wore a navy polo and khaki rousers. The transformation those effected surprised her, aaking him seem almost a stranger.

An officer and a gentleman. The familiar phrase reverber-ted, making her realize that Major Jacob Underwood was ndoubtedly more sophisticated than she'd given him credit or.

"I can make coffee." She wasn't sure where that offer had ome from. Maybe from the sense of absolute aloneness she ad felt watching the steam rise off her cooling bathwater.

"I don't know what kind of reception an uninvited guest s supposed to receive down here," he said, "but whatever it s, don't feel under any obligation to provide it. I shouldn't ave said what I did to you this afternoon. No one could have one more than you have with this. And it isn't really even our job. That's what the FBI is here for. If, with all their esources, they can't find Raine Nolan, no one expects you) do it."

"No one but me," Eden said. "And you were right before. It *my* job. This is my town and my people, and I'm responsible or what happens to them. I feel that very strongly."

"I know. I said what I did because I was angry, not because think you haven't been doing all you can."

"I appreciate that. Look, if you don't want coffee, how

about tea? You can have it hot or iced." He had begun to shake
his head, but she plowed on, unready to face her dilemma
again. "Since I haven't eaten today, I was about to make
myself a sandwich. I hate to eat alone."

He would think she was coming on to him. At this point
she didn't particularly care if he did. *As long as he stayed.*

She needed someone to talk to. Someone intelligent and
rational, and less emotionally involved in this than she was

*Like the guy who claims to have visions of missing chil
dren?*

She pushed that unwanted thought out of her head, waiting
for him to turn her down. He surprised her instead.

"Okay. And I drink my tea iced."

"Fair enough." She started toward the kitchen and realized
she was still holding the Glock. As she passed the couch, she
pushed the weapon back into its holster.

"You always answer the door armed?"

"I've never felt the need to before tonight. Someone broke
into my house today. I discovered that fact as I was undressing
to take my bath. Right before you rang the bell."

His pupils widened into the surrounding ring of gray. And
then he asked the pertinent question. "You're sure they're not
still here?"

She nodded. "I checked."

"You think it was somebody from this morning?"

He meant one of the men who had attacked him, she re
alized, something that had never crossed her mind. Would
one of them be so angry she'd interrupted their fun that he'd
decided to play a prank on her? Except...

"I wouldn't think so."

His face changed, concern replaced by confusion.
"Then...? You have any idea what they were after? Was any
thing taken?"

She shook her head. "That's what I need to talk about. To
try to figure out what this was all about."

"What you *need* to do is get some of your people out here to dust for prints. They also need to check for footprints outside. Look for forced entry. You *know* what you need to be doing."

"There won't be any prints. Just like there weren't any on Lincoln Greene's truck."

"You think this is the same guy who came out to my place and took a shot at you?"

She nodded. "I'm sure of it. Look, I don't know about you, but I'm going to need something to keep me awake and lucid. We can talk while we eat." She gestured toward the door to the kitchen.

His gaze followed, at least briefly, before it came back to her face. "How'd you know someone had been here?"

She didn't want to go back into the bedroom. The feeling was visceral. Gut level. Patently ridiculous. And exactly the same as when she'd seen the gingham quilt.

"I'll show you."

As he followed her down the darkened hallway, she was conscious for the first time of how little she was wearing underneath her robe. And very conscious of how thin was the fabric from which it was made.

She stopped at the door of the bedroom, steeling herself to enter. Instead, Jake brushed by her and, guided by the lamp she hadn't turned off, walked straight to the side of the bed where the doll lay.

He studied it for a moment, before he turned back to her. "You think somebody's taunting you? Because we haven't found her yet?"

We. We haven't found her yet.

Was he sensitive enough to know how accusatory "you" would have felt in that sentence? Or did he, too, feel this crushing sense of responsibility?

"Actually…I don't think that's supposed to represent Raine."

"Then…" He shook his head again. "I don't understand. What the hell's going on?"

"That's what I wanted to talk to you about. To explain what I think this is. This *and* the quilt."

"The *quilt?* The one in the truck."

She nodded. "I don't think either of them has anything to do with Raine." She stopped, because she couldn't say that with any certitude. "At least… It's complicated. That's why I'd like to talk it all out with somebody who…somebody who can view it with some kind of detachment. Who can think rationally about what's happening."

"And you believe I'm that person."

The confusion in his voice had been replaced by some emotion she couldn't identify.

"Yes."

As she'd stood in the bathroom, she had considered the very limited list of people she might trust with this. Dean should have been at the top, but she knew how he would react. Just as he'd reacted to Jake's story.

Next had been Doc Murphy, who was not only the county coroner, but had been her father's doctor, as well. And for that reason alone she had rejected him.

She had even briefly considered the minister at the church she attended, but in her opinion, this wasn't going to be the kind of situation one turned to the clergy to solve.

Now, instead of trusting any of them, she was about to reveal more about herself than she had ever told those other people to a man who had more right than anyone else to refuse her plea for help. The one man who would be fully justified in telling her to leave him the hell alone.

And that he hadn't done that—at least not yet—made her know she'd made the right decision.

Chapter Eleven

Eden had poured the iced tea she'd promised, but she seemed to have forgotten that she needed to eat. They were sitting now at the scarred wooden table in her small kitchen.

Jake watched as she ran her finger around the rim of her untouched cup of coffee while she talked. The motion was unthinking, unconscious, as the past slowly unfolded in her mind's eye. Even the cadence of her speech seemed to have slipped into a more childish rhythm.

"I was two years older than Christie. That meant I was supposed to look after her. I can hear my mother's voice saying that to this day. 'Look after your sister, Edie. Make sure nothing happens to her.'

"We'd been swimming that day. Mama had taken us by herself because Daddy had to work. We went to the community pool, like always. There must have been two hundred people there. It was a Saturday, so it was mostly families. Lots of kids. I had trouble keeping an eye on Christie. She kept running into the women's locker room, she said to go to the bathroom. She'd do that everywhere she went. Daddy said she was taking a survey of all the bathrooms in the state." Her lips tilted at the memory, and then the smile faded as she went on with her story.

"Mama would send me into the locker room to get her because she'd be gone so long. Once when I went in, she wasn't there. I searched everywhere, all over the building, but when I went to tell Mama I couldn't find her, Christie was in the pool. I didn't say anything to Mama, afraid I'd get her in trouble, but then I wondered, after it happened—"

She stopped, lifting her eyes to his. "Sorry. I know…" She shook her head. "It's been so long. And I've never talked about this. I've tried not to think about it."

"Just take your time," Jake said soothingly.

This wasn't something he wanted to hear, and he didn't understand how some incident from her childhood had anything to do with someone breaking into her house or with Raine Nolan. Since she seemed to feel it was somehow connected, he was at least willing to listen and then draw his own conclusions.

Eden took a breath, her finger again beginning that slow circle around her cup. "We were tired. Playing in the water does that to you. And the heat. After supper, Mama sent us up to bed. I don't think either of us made a fuss, but it must have been early. Not even dark yet. That didn't keep me from falling asleep, almost as soon as my head touched the pillow. I don't know about Christie, but she didn't usually get out of bed. Of course, she had been so bad at the pool…" The sentence trailed as she appeared to consider whether or not her sister might have continued her misbehavior that night.

"When I woke up the next morning, the sun was so bright coming in through the curtains, my first thought was that someone should have called me because it was so late. I lay there and listened a long time, but I couldn't hear Mama down in the kitchen. The house was too quiet, like everyone had gotten up and gone someplace and left me asleep.

"But it was Sunday. And Mama wouldn't dream of not going to church. When I looked over at Christie's bed, I knew she wasn't there. I could always see the lump she made under the sheet, but it wasn't there that morning. I thought maybe she'd gone down to wake up Mama and Daddy. I thought…"

She shook her head again. "*Nothing* bad. Nothing bad had ever happened in my whole life. Not before that morning. And I had no reason to expect that anything ever would."

She looked up again, her eyes bright with unshed tears. "Even after all this time, I can remember what I felt when I walked over to the bed and saw Christie's baby doll tucked under the sheet. I thought she was playing a trick on me. Like she had at the pool the day before. I thought she was hiding somewhere. Trying to scare me. Or that she was down in the kitchen, eating the leftover brownies Mama had made for our picnic the day before. The thought that she could really be gone—that someone had come into our house and taken her—never crossed my mind. Things like that didn't happen. Not to my family. Or my sister."

Eden stopped again, and Jake waited through the silence, knowing now where this was leading. Even to the quilt and the doll.

And then, after a long time, she went on, hurrying now, as if she just wanted the telling to be over. "But she wasn't downstairs. Mama and Daddy were still asleep. Just worn out, he always said. And none of us had heard a thing. I was in the same room with her, and I never heard a sound.

"Somebody had taken my sister. They wrapped her in the quilt my grandmother had made for her christening. And they put that baby doll in her place. And we never saw her again."

The painful narrative seemed to have ground to a halt. Jake wasn't sure what to say. Or what to ask.

She had wanted to tell him this, so he could offer a rational explanation for why, during another kidnapping years later, motifs from her sister's kidnapping were being repeated. But he had no explanation. Not one that made any kind of sense.

"Are you saying that was your sister's quilt? The one in the truck?"

"It wasn't. It was machine-made. New. But...it *looked*

almost the same. And I don't understand how *anyone* could have known that."

"How it looked?"

"That there even was a quilt. Or a kidnapping. My daddy never talked about her. I didn't. When we left Ohio, we came here to get away from those memories. We never told anybody here what had happened."

"You can't know that for sure." She'd been a child. She wouldn't have been privy to everything her parents did or said. "What about your mother? Women find comfort in talking about tragedies."

He sounded like some psychology text. Where did he get off telling her what women found comfort in?

"My mother didn't. Maybe if she had… She never got over losing Christie. She kept thinking that one day she'd come home. They wrapped her in her quilt, she'd say, so she wouldn't be cold. Surely that means they're taking good care of her. Everybody commented on the fact that she was being so brave. That she never lost hope. And then one night she took my father's service revolver and put it to her temple and pulled the trigger."

The quiet words were more chilling somehow because there was so little emotion in them. First she had lost her sister. And then her mother. How did someone survive something like that and emerge on the other side sane and whole?

"Daddy blamed himself for that, too," she added softly.

"Too?"

"He blamed himself for losing Christie. He was her father. He was supposed to protect her. I knew *exactly* what Ray Nolan was feeling Monday morning. I could see it in his eyes. The same look that was in my father's until the day he died."

Jake couldn't think of anything to say to that, but the silence that followed became unbearable, so that he asked the question he'd wondered about since he'd met Eden Reddick.

"Is that why you went into law enforcement? To keep that from happening to another family?"

She looked up from her concentration on the rim of her cup to answer him. "If it was, it doesn't seem as if my career path has been particularly successful."

"I told you. I don't know what else you could be doing. Or what else anyone could do."

"Forgive me, but right now—and as long as Raine's missing—that's cold comfort."

"You think her disappearance is connected to your sister's?"

She shook her head. "Another kidnapping twenty years later? I wouldn't think so."

"What's to say he hasn't done this a dozen times since he took your sister? In a dozen other places?"

"You ask if my sister was the reason I went into law enforcement. She wasn't. But…I think that was my father's motivation. He saw it as a way to get information. To see if there were similar cases out there. Although he tried to find those from the first time he pinned on his badge, that kind of search has gotten a lot easier for law enforcement in the last ten or fifteen years. Before my father died, he had access to most of the national crime databases. The public search engines. The files of every major newspaper. And believe me, he took advantage of all of them."

"Are you saying he didn't find any other kidnapping like your sister's?" Jake found it hard to believe that. He could think of a couple that had gotten coverage on the major networks that were enough alike to make anyone suspicious.

"A few with enough elements in common to make him contact the agencies in charge. But there was always something about each of them that made him believe it couldn't be the same guy who'd taken Christie. And if there was a suspect in custody, he'd go through channels to get permission to speak to them. Most of the time, departments will arrange that as a courtesy to officers with open cases if they can. The fact that *his* daughter was the victim may have made them more accommodating. But no matter how hopeful he was going into those situations, he'd always come home and say the same thing. "'Not this time, Edie. But he's out there. I know he's out there.'"

"You think he really believed that?"

"That her kidnapper was still alive somewhere?"

"That none of the others were the work of the same guy."

"I think…" Her finger began its slow journey again. "I think he never gave up hope of finding her. All those other cases…" Her voice rose on the last word. "*None* of those little girls survived. Not for more than a few days." She looked up to meet his eyes once more. "To my father, that meant their kidnapper couldn't have been the same person who took Christie, because that meant Christie was no longer alive."

"And you don't believe her kidnapper took Raine, either. Then why the quilt and the doll?"

"I think those were directed at me."

"Why?"

"Some kind of sadistic mind game. Maybe to bring it all back. To interfere with the investigation. I don't know."

"How would they know to do that? You said your father never talked about what happened to your sister."

"Not here. Not in town. But he *did* talk. To the FBI. To cold-case divisions all over the country. To law-enforcement agencies that were involved in any case that had something in common with Christie's."

"And you think one of *those* people is pulling these Halloween pranks?"

"Is that what you think they are? Pranks?"

"There aren't all that many options."

"What does that mean?"

"Somebody's trying to rattle you, using objects associated with your sister's disappearance. What are your choices as to who's doing it? Her kidnapper? Raine's kidnapper? Someone connected to neither? Or someone connected to both?"

"I don't understand. Who could be connected to both?"

"You for one."

Her eyes widened. "I didn't—"

"I know. I didn't mean that you had anything to do with what's going on. But the possibility exists that you aren't the only one with ties to both cases. The possibility also exists that someone is using your sister's disappearance to interfere with your investigation of Raine's. Maybe they're trying to make you believe there's a connection when there isn't."

"Why would they do that?"

"Just what I said. To interfere with what you're trying to do."

"I'm *trying* to find Raine," she said softly. "And the only person who should want to interfere with that—"

"Would be whoever has taken her," he finished for her.

Chapter Twelve

"I never got around to making you that sandwich I promised."

Eden had walked him to the front door, although she seemed almost reluctant for him to leave. Remembering that she'd carried her weapon when she let him in, Jake wondered if she was nervous about being in the house alone.

Not that he was going to volunteer to spend the night. It had been temptation enough sitting across the table from her the past hour.

"You want me to check the house before I leave?" he offered.

"Whoever was here is long gone. I'll be fine."

He started to tell her to call him if she was afraid, but that was another bad idea. Despite the anger he'd felt toward Eden this afternoon, she was the first woman he'd been attracted to in a very long time. Hell, she was the first woman he'd been *around* in a long time.

Maybe the strongly sexual pull he felt right now had something to do with the vulnerability that talking about her sister's kidnapping had revealed, but there was no denying Eden Reddick was a very beautiful woman. And the fact that she seemed determined not to let the home invasion spook her only increased his admiration.

"Even so," he said, "lock up when I leave."

"Unlike most of Waverly, I always do," she assured him, as she opened the door to see him out.

A car was turning into her drive, its headlights illuminating the back of Jake's truck, parked out on the street. They watched together as Eden's deputy chief got out from behind the wheel and started up the sidewalk.

"What's wrong?" Eden called.

Jake could feel her tension. Apparently, her second-in-command didn't customarily come calling at night. A situation in which Jake took an unwarranted satisfaction.

"One of the teams found something you'll want to see," Partlow said, as he climbed the steps. He nodded to Jake, his eyes full of speculation, before he turned back to Eden. "Everything all right here?"

"It's not Raine, is it?" Eden asked, instead of answering his question. "Is she dead?"

"I'd have told you if she was. This is…" Partlow looked at Jake again. "We think it may be where he kept her."

"Underground," Jake guessed, knowing that it would pain the deputy to be forced to admit that. "Some kind of bunker."

"If I were you, I wouldn't gloat too much about being right," Partlow warned. "Folks around here are already convinced you know a little too much about all this."

"Where?" Eden demanded, cutting through the exchange.

"Out on Diggstown Road. Some of Gulf State Paper's property."

"What does that mean?" Jake asked.

"Paper companies own a lot of the land down here. Some they grant public access to for hunting or fishing. Some they don't," the deputy explained. "That doesn't mean people don't do those things on the property."

"It isn't guarded," Eden added. "Most of the time there aren't even gates on the roads through it, although they're marked private."

"So you're saying that anybody could have gotten out there?" Jake asked.

"Anybody who was aware of all those things," Partlow agreed.

"And that would be almost everybody who'd ever lived around here."

The flatness of Eden's voice verified what Jake had already figured out. This bunker, or whatever it was, wasn't going to be the breakthrough they'd been hoping for. Nothing that would narrow down their search for the Nolan child's kidnapper beyond the few thousand or so residents of the town.

"I'd like to see it." Jake looked to Eden for permission. Despite the deputy's description, he wasn't sure if this was the place he'd seen in that first flashback, or whether it was what to him had seemed a more permanent structure in the later one.

"Crime scene," Partlow declared. "We're keeping the public away, so as not to contaminate whatever evidence might be out there."

Ignoring that authoritative directive, Jake made his appeal to Eden. "I can tell you if this is the place he took her first. That might be helpful information to have further into the investigation."

"Chief, we don't have time for this right now. We got a crime scene and the possibility of finding something that might lead us to whoever took that little girl."

"I think I'd like to know." Eden's voice was decisive. Despite her bathrobe and bare feet, she, at least, seemed to have no doubt who was in charge. "Major Underwood's right. It might be helpful at some point to know which this is."

"Information based on his visions. Is that what you're saying, Chief?"

"I'm saying that I think it's a good idea if Major Underwood rides along. I'd like to have his impressions of what they found out there. It won't take me a minute to throw some clothes on. We'll take my car and follow you."

It was as neat a dismissal as Jake had ever seen. She denied the deputy's arguments without ignoring his concerns. And Partlow's resentment of her exertion of authority was apparent in every step he took on the way back to the police cruiser.

"Thanks," Jake said, when Dean was out of earshot. "I don't think your deputy was happy with your decision."

"Dean?" Eden seemed surprised. "I don't know why he should care if you come. Once the evidence techs get through out there, everybody and his brother is going to show up to sightsee. And by morning, when the media finds out, it'll be nothing short of a sideshow."

JAKE HADN'T SAID much since they'd arrived at the scene. Intent on examining every part of the hole that had been tunneled out of the Mississippi clay, Eden hadn't even noticed when he'd disappeared back up the primitive wooden ladder that allowed access to the earthen cavity. When she had asked Dean where he'd gone, the deputy had shrugged, but the grin on his face had told her he had his own ideas about that.

As soon as she emerged from the bunker, she spotted Jake standing apart from the crowd of deputies and agents who had gathered, despite the lateness of the hour. Fielding questions and comments as she walked, Eden approached him, aware that their meeting would be watched with interest by the assembly.

"What do you think?"

"She was here."

"You're sure."

He nodded, the gray eyes bleak.

"Is this where he brought her first?" There wasn't much doubt in her mind of that, based on the description he'd given of exposed roots and dripping water. Anyone who had listened to Jake that first day couldn't fail to see the similarities.

Something about his stillness bothered her. Was he again sensing the child's terror? Or was there something else going on? Something Jake felt, but didn't want to articulate?

"What's wrong?" She deliberately kept her voice low, so it wouldn't carry to those who were pretending not to listen.

"He had to have spent a lot of time out here. Getting that ready."

She nodded, unsure where he was going with this.

"Yet I haven't seen him in any of the flashbacks. I think she heard him in the second one, but…" He shook his head, his eyes still empty.

"You've thought from the first that your connection was with her."

"A time and place."

"What?"

"That's what a flashback is. A particular time and place. So why isn't he ever here?"

She had no answer for that. She wasn't even sure she understood what he was getting at.

Before she had time to formulate a response, out of the corner of her eye she caught someone moving purposefully through the crowd gathered around the entrance to the bunker. Someone *not* wearing a uniform.

As she turned to identify that person, Ray Nolan was approaching Dean. Although Eden was too far away to hear what they said, there was no doubt from his downward gesture what Raine's father wanted. Dean seemed to argue briefly, but eventually Ray got his way, disappearing into the bunker where, at least briefly, his daughter had apparently been hidden.

"I probably need to be over there when he comes up," she said to Jake.

Although he nodded agreement, she was still bothered enough by his uncharacteristic behavior to ask, "Is there something else you think we ought to be doing about this?"

"You? No."

There wasn't time for anything else, because Ray was emerging from the bunker. He made a beeline for where she and Jake were standing. Eden walked forward to meet him, unsure how he would react to Underwood being here.

"Is this it?" Ray asked, as he approached. "Is this the place he described to you?"

It was obvious he was upset, but she still wasn't sure whether that was from seeing where the kidnapper had held Raine, or because they'd allowed Jake to be present at the scene. Just to be sure it wasn't the latter, she tried to step between Ray and the ex-soldier, but Nolan pushed her aside.

"They may be gullible enough to believe you knew about this from some kind of vision, but I'm not. Where the hell is my daughter, you bastard?"

Anger overcoming his control, Ray lunged at Jake. Eden attempted to step between them again. Once more, Raine's father shoved her, hard enough this time to slam her into a nearby pine.

Ignoring the pain in her shoulder, she tried to get her hand around Ray's arm to restrain him. Jake's move was more effective. He took Nolan's outstretched wrist and used it to spin the man around, pinning his arm high behind his back.

Then, the movement almost faster than she could follow, Jake's other forearm snaked around Ray's neck, forcing the smaller man's head back against his shoulder. Nolan struggled briefly against the hold, but the ex-soldier jacked his arm higher, easily controlling him with the very real threat of a dislocated shoulder.

"You ever hit a woman again, and I'll come after you," Jake ground out. "You hear me?"

When the man he held refused to answer, he tightened the pressure until Raine's father cried out. "You understand?" Jake demanded again.

Ray nodded, unable to prevent an accompanying whimper

of pain. Taking that for agreement, apparently, Jake released him, pushing him forward so violently that he almost fell.

"I don't give a damn whether you believe me or not. I saw a little girl in one of my flashbacks. She was in a place that looked like that hole down there. That's what I told the police. And that's the sum total of what I know about your daughter."

It was obvious Ray would like to have argued the point. Luckily, the ease with which he'd just been manhandled convinced him not to.

"If you had anything—"

"He didn't," Eden interrupted. "If he had, do you honestly believe he would have come to us with that story? Why would he tell us about this place if he's the one who built it? That makes no sense, and you know it, Ray."

"So where is she?" Nolan's challenge was addressed to Jake. "You claim you can see her, so where the hell is she now?"

"That's enough, Ray," Eden urged.

"Seems you can't make him tell you all he knows, Chief. But there are people in this town who could. I guarantee you that."

Eden ignored the muttered agreement from someone in the crowd of deputies and agents. "And *I* guarantee that you *and* those people better stick to what you know and let law enforcement do their job."

"Then *do* it, damn it. Find my baby girl. Until you do, we got nothing else to talk about."

Nolan stooped to pick up the baseball cap Jake's choke hold had dislodged. Hat in hand, he stalked across the area roped off by yellow crime-scene tape. The officers watching parted to let him pass, but none of them spoke to him.

Eden turned to look at Jake, who was still watching Ray's departure. "You did say you didn't need protection. I guess I should have taken you at your word."

His gaze came back to her. "I can't blame him for what

he thinks. I don't know how to explain what I saw. I don't understand it myself."

"Whatever happened, you were right about this."

"Somehow I don't think many of them…" His eyes lifted to the men still gathered around the opening of the bunker he'd so accurately described. "I don't think they buy that I saw this any way other than how we're seeing it tonight."

She couldn't deny that. Dean had been in the office the first time Jake had told his story. And he remained unconvinced.

"Whether they buy it or not, we all need to begin looking for the second location. You need to make a sketch of what you saw. We can print it up and distribute it to the teams."

"Would something like a sketch have helped you find this?" His disbelief was patent.

"We gave the teams instructions to look for something *exactly* like this. They might have overlooked the subtle signs that the ground had been disturbed here if we hadn't done that."

Jake's gaze returned to the group gathered around the bunker. "It's been nearly twenty-four hours."

He meant since he'd had the flashback involving a second location. And they both knew that was an eternity in a kidnapping case.

She understood that Jake's greatest fear was the same as hers. That he hadn't had another flashback since because whatever connection had allowed them had now been broken. The most obvious reason for that would be…

She denied the thought, just as she had denied it for the past five days. "I know," she comforted him. "But right now, we just don't have anything else."

Chapter Thirteen

It was well after midnight before the technicians were finished. Whatever their previous intentions, it seemed the agents wouldn't be headed back to Jackson this morning.

Although Eden was no longer in charge of the examination of the bunker the searchers had discovered, she had wanted to be with the techs as they looked for anything that might give them a clue as to who'd dug the pit.

A pit that matched, in almost every detail, Jake Underwood's description that first day. Yet, in the intervening hours, she had almost forgotten he'd come with her to the site.

When she reached the top of the wooden ladder, she immediately looked for him, but couldn't find him among the few lingering onlookers. Her first thought was that he'd caught a ride home with someone else. Considering the opinion of most of the townspeople, and that included the men in her department, she realized how unlikely that would be.

As she headed toward her cruiser, she noted each knot of men she passed. Several people spoke to her, asking some variation of the question that was on everyone's mind: *Anything left behind in the bunker that might lead them to the kidnapper?*

Jake was not among any of the groups. Although Ray Nolan looked up as she walked by, he didn't speak, apparently still angered that she'd denied him permission to torture Jake into a confession.

But she was too tired to muster any charitable feelings, even for Raine's father. And certainly not for any of the others who believed they could do a better job of handling this.

As she opened the door of the patrol car, the overhead light illuminated Jake sitting in the passenger seat, which had been tilted into a reclining position. She couldn't tell if he'd been asleep, because he straightened at once, returning the seat to its upright position.

"I wondered where you'd gotten to," she said, climbing into the driver's seat.

"The good citizens of Waverly seemed less welcoming than usual."

"I can imagine."

Actually, she didn't have to imagine. The animosity emanating from the crowd as Ray made his accusations had been thick enough to cut with a knife.

"Is this what you had in mind?" He held out the notepad she always kept in her car.

On the top sheet Jake had done the sketch she'd asked for. The quality of the pencil drawing was professional. Almost artistic. And, most important, highly detailed.

"More than I was hoping for, actually. I wasn't sure from what you said about the scene whether you could produce anything that might be helpful."

As the words came out of her mouth, she felt a frisson of unease. Not quite distrust, it was more like confusion.

Jake had seemed almost as vague about the particulars of the second location as he had been the first time he'd described the bunker. This drawing, however...

"It came back to me as I worked. Like not remembering the exposed roots until I got to the caves. When I started this—" he lifted the notebook to bring her attention back to it "—the picture was all there, waiting inside my head."

"It's very good." It was. And if it was accurate, it might well lead them to where he had seen the child in the second flashback.

"They find anything?"

"What?" Her attention still on the sketch, for a moment she wasn't sure what he meant.

"In the bunker. Was there anything there that might tell you who dug it?"

"They'll collect everything that could do that, but…" She shook her head. "I don't know."

"You need to get some sleep."

She laughed. "I *need* to do a lot of things."

"Whatever they found tonight will have to be processed. There's nothing you can do until that's finished."

"Ray didn't seem to think."

"His little girl is missing. He isn't thinking at all right now."

"I know. I'd be crazed. My father was. I'm not sure he ever recovered."

She took the pad from his hand, laying it on the seat between them, and started the cruiser. She didn't try to make conversation as she maneuvered between the cars belonging to the officers working the scene.

When they were once more out on the highway, she said what she had failed to say earlier. "By the way, thank you for defending me tonight."

"Defending you?"

"When Ray shoved me. It wasn't necessary, but…I appreciated it all the same."

"I wanted to beat him to a pulp," Jake said.

Doc Murphy had talked about the impulsiveness and anger-management issues that were so often a part of a brain injury. Beating Ray to a pulp certainly sounded like the latter.

"Then I also appreciate that you didn't do it. I'm too tired to face the paperwork that would have necessitated." She turned to smile at him, hoping her warning was subtle enough not to offend.

After all, despite that vaunted Southern chivalry people made so much of, it wasn't often a man came to her rescue. She was the chief of police. She was supposed to be able to take care of herself.

"Your deputy said I needed to file charges against the guy this morning."

"Dave Porter." Once more she had forgotten about that. "You don't *have* to, but we can't hold him any longer unless you do. I think Dean arrested him on a public-disturbance charge. But as the damaged party, you'll need to file the assault charges."

"Is that what you want?"

"He seemed to be the ring leader of the attack," she acknowledged. "It might be good to let him cool his heels a few more days. Mind you, I'm not an unbiased observer. Street fights require paperwork, too."

"I'll do it tomorrow. Will you be in the office?"

She glanced at him in surprise. "After they found that bunker? Every media outlet in the country will have someone down here. And most of them will want to talk to me. Too bad the department doesn't have a PR person. I could use one right now."

"No one else articulate enough to handle them?"

"If that's a compliment, thanks. If it's a kind way of suggesting I need to see if there's anyone else, you're probably right."

"You've done a good job. Given the circumstances, it can't have been easy."

"It isn't. Dean's handled some of the requests for information or interviews, but he'd rather be out with the search teams. Or dealing with the FBI. And that's good by me. They're more comfortable with him."

"Because you're a woman."

It hadn't been a question, but she treated it as one. "I guess. They think they have to watch their language. You can almost see them mentally searching for an alternate way to say the things they normally say without thinking about them."

"I've been in that situation myself."

She glanced over to see if that hint of amusement she'd heard in his voice was reflected in his expression. As she did, he turned to meet her eyes.

Even in the dark interior of the car, she was jolted by what she saw in his. She quickly returned her gaze to the road, trying to decide if she'd really seen what she thought she had.

Except there wasn't much that could be mistaken for that particular look. She eased a breath, thinking about the ramifications of allowing anything to happen between them. Half the town thought he was involved in Raine's kidnapping. The other half thought he was just a guy who was a couple of cards short of a full deck. And while she didn't think either of those assessments was accurate, what did she really know about Jake Underwood?

Even as she posed the question, she enumerated the answers. That he was a decorated veteran. Intelligent. Well mannered. From a good family. Something that still mattered probably more than it should down here.

And all of which had at one time or another been said about half of the most notorious serial killers.

"You okay?"

Jake's question interrupted that unwanted bit of introspection. No matter what she thought or felt about him, this was neither the time nor the place to get involved with anyone. Much less someone her town considered a prime suspect.

"If I don't sleep soon, I'm going to make one of those mistakes you regret all your life."

But it's not going to be getting involved with a man I know virtually nothing about.

"You're almost home."

They were, she realized. Apparently, she'd been driving by rote, following the familiar roads without consciously thinking about any of them.

She concentrated on them now, aware once more, as the adrenaline from tonight's find faded, of how exhausted she was. As she turned onto her street, her headlights picked up Jake's truck, still parked in front of her house. She pulled into the driveway and turned off the engine.

It felt as if there was something more that should be said between them, but she was too drained to think what it might be. All she wanted was to get out of her clothes and crawl into bed.

The one where the taunting baby doll still rested its head on her pillow.

After all that had happened in the past few days, why would a doll in her bed feel like some kind of insurmountable problem? "I'm not sure I can do this," she admitted.

"The investigation?"

She didn't look at Jake, knowing that, as experienced at reading people as he was, he would see through any pretense she might make, straight to her fear and weakness.

"Go inside," she whispered finally. "Inside that house. Inside that room."

He didn't respond. After a few seconds, she heard him open his door and then close it, blessedly switching off the too-revealing overhead light.

Then her door opened and Jake put his hand under her elbow. "Come on."

"I can't."

"You don't have to. I'll take care of it. Just get out of the car. That's all you have to do. Get out and walk inside."

"Not by myself?" she asked softly, hearing the pleading in her own voice.

"No, not by yourself."

JAKE HAD SEEN IT before in combat. Too much stress. Too little sleep. The body protects itself by giving up, even as the mind refuses to acknowledge the breakdown.

He had thought about trying to get her into the shower before he put her to bed, but decided that was tempting fate. In more ways than one.

Instead, he left her in the hall while he retrieved the nightgown he'd noticed on the foot of her bed when she'd brought him in to see the doll. He put the gown into her hands and then guided her toward the bathroom with instructions to undress.

Then he walked back across the hall. He stood a moment looking down on the object in her bed, resisting the urge to open a window and throw it out. Instead, he pulled down the top sheet and the quilt, until he could see the entire surface of the bed.

There were no more surprises. Apparently, the bastard who'd left it had been satisfied with just the doll. Not that it hadn't been effective.

The water began running across the hall, reminding him that he had only a couple of minutes to turn this horror show into a place where Eden could rest. He lifted the pillow under the plastic head, allowing the doll to slide onto the mattress. Then he removed the pillowcase, using that to pick up the doll, which he laid on the dresser.

In a matter of seconds, he had stripped the bed, piling the linens at its foot. He found clean sheets in the second place he looked, on the top shelf of her closet. He made the bed quickly, employing skills that had been drummed into him years ago in basic training.

Conscious that precious seconds were ticking away, he decided to take care of the doll before he replaced the quilt. As he gathered up the bedding, he heard the door across the hall open. Hurrying now, he carried the load of sheets in his arms to the dresser and dumped them on top of the doll.

When he turned, Eden was standing in the doorway. "That's a *very* impressive hospital corner."

"We prefer the term 'army corner.' I just need to replace the quilt."

He picked it up off the floor and shook it out before he allowed it to settle over the clean sheets. He didn't bother to tuck it in, but he did turn the covers down on the opposite side from where the doll had lain.

"Get in. I'll be back in a minute to turn out the light."

Without waiting to see if she obeyed, he picked up the sheets he'd removed from the bed, making sure they still concealed the doll. He walked across the hall and laid the pile on the bathroom counter.

He opened the medicine cabinet, making a quick survey of its contents. He selected a bottle of an OTC painkiller/sleep aid and poured two tablets into his palm.

When he returned to the bedroom, carrying the medication and a glass of water, only the bedside lamp that had been on the first time she'd brought him here was still burning.

Eden watched him cross the room. Her eyes widened as he held the tablets out on his palm. "What is that?"

"Something to help you sleep."

Her laugh was a breath of sound. "I don't think I'll need any help sleeping."

"With these, you won't dream."

She hesitated, her eyes holding his. "I have to be at the department in the morning."

"I know. I'll wake you."

After a second, she took the pills off his hand and put them into her mouth. He held out the glass, which she drank down as if she had realized only now that she was thirsty.

"You aren't leaving." Her eyes pled with him, even if her tone did not.

"I'll be right here." He took the glass out of her hand. "And you'll wake me in time."

"I'll wake you. Now go to sleep. You can't afford any mistakes tomorrow, remember."

She nodded and then watched again as he rounded the bed toward the lamp on the other side. He put his fingers on the switch, but before he turned it, he asked, "Did you keep your father's research? The stuff he collected on the other kidnappings?"

"Of course."

"Is it here?"

This time, as she nodded, a small crease had formed between her brows. Clearly, she was trying to figure out where he was going with this.

"I'd like to look at it. If that's okay with you."

"I told you. He didn't find anything that matched—" She stopped, realizing what he intended to do. "You think another case like *this* one may be in there."

"I think it's worth a look. And since I'm going to be here…" He shrugged.

"They're in the closet in his bedroom. I can help." She began to push back the covers.

"Not tonight. Tonight you sleep. If I find anything I think might be relevant, you'll be the first to know, I promise you." As he said the last, he turned the switch, plunging the room into darkness.

It was time to go. Time to get out of her bedroom and to spend the night exactly as he'd told her he would.

And past time to disabuse himself of the notion that someone as put together as Eden Reddick could ever be interested in someone with as much baggage as he carried.

They had told him when he'd been commissioned that he was an officer and a gentleman. He'd always tried to live up to both standards. He had every intention of doing that tonight.

Except he knew very well which road was paved with those kinds of intentions.

Chapter Fourteen

Eden opened her eyes to sunlight filtering in around her bedroom curtains. The bedside clock read 7:30, at least an hour later than she normally got up. Still early enough, she assured herself, to grab a shower and make it in before the media began questioning why she wasn't there to talk about yesterday's discovery.

With that thought came the memory of Jake asking to see her father's files and promising to wake her. The fact that he hadn't might indicate he had left with the sunrise. Or it might simply mean he knew how much she had needed this sleep.

For the first time in days, she felt as if she could take time to think things through without someone believing she was falling down on her job. And the first thing she needed to think about was a statement.

It was always possible Dean had already taken care of that. A task she was more than willing to hand off to her second-in-command. She just didn't believe he would attempt to do it without consulting her. Which meant…

She threw back the covers and crawled out of bed. In case Jake was still in the house, she gathered up every item of clothing she would need for the day before she walked across to the bathroom.

She couldn't tell whether or not she was alone by the quality of the silence that greeted her. Only the fragrance of coffee that permeated the air told her that, whatever else Jake might have accomplished last night, he'd kept his promise. He had stood guard over her as she'd slept, just as he'd said he would.

As soon as she was decent, she would thank him for that, as well as for the caffeine. Despite having slept longer last night than she'd managed during the past four days combined, she knew she badly needed the stimulus a couple of cups of coffee would provide.

Fifteen minutes later she emerged from the bathroom, showered, dressed and wearing makeup. She refused to examine too closely why she had felt the last was necessary, chalking up the impulse to giving her confidence a boost as she faced the cameras.

When she entered the kitchen she found her breakfast table buried under mounds of folders. Although they seemed to be arranged in stacks, her initial impression was one of chaos. Whatever hope she might have had for some breakthrough as a result of Jake's search through her father's documents quickly faded.

"Good morning." Jake verbally acknowledged her presence, but his eyes remained focused on the pages spread out in front of him.

"Thanks for staying. And for making coffee." Not exactly the speech she had planned, but since he didn't seem particularly interested in what she had to say, she decided it would do.

"How'd you sleep?" He looked up this time, eyes narrowed slightly against the sunlight that streamed into the room through the window over the sink.

It illuminated his face: the angles of his cheekbones, the strength of his jawline, the shape of his mouth. Eden's heart stopped. *Literally.*

And although it quickly resumed an almost regular rhythm, she knew that her uneventfully small-town existence had just taken another turn. One as potentially life-altering as the crime that had changed everything she had once believed about Waverly.

Jake's eyes appeared blue, rather than their normal gray. A trick of the light? Or a reflection from the navy polo he wore?

All she knew was that the difference between their color and the deep tan of the face that surrounded them was stunning. The growth of dark whiskers covering his cheeks pointed up that contrast, as did the midnight gleam of his hair.

Perhaps because she had at first considered him nothing more than a suspect and then, only later, an ally, she was shocked to realize now how breathtakingly handsome she found a man she had never thought of in that light.

Blatantly masculine, yes. She had acknowledged that from the day he'd walked into her office. It would be hard not to, given the testosterone-laden confidence with which he'd carried himself, despite the limp. But handsome?

"Eden?"

Hearing her name brought her out of the shattering fog of self-discovery. She was attracted to Jake Underwood.

Not because of his intellect or his service record or the way he had handled himself from the beginning of all this. Or maybe because of all of those.

And at some point she would have to deal with her feelings. Just not while he was sitting at her kitchen table.

"So, what did you find?" The tone of her question was too bright. As if they were talking about the weather. Or a book they'd both read. Not the search for a terrified child.

"Several things I'd like to look at a little more closely."

That didn't sound encouraging, but then she hadn't expected him to discover Raine's kidnapper lurking among her father's yellowing papers.

"Of course. You want to take them with you?"

"Maybe. I haven't even finished going through everything. Your dad was nothing if not thorough."

"I told you. He was... I guess *obsessed* is fair. He really thought that if he looked hard enough..." She blocked the memory of all those nights she'd watched her father pore over these same documents. "I have to go. There are eggs and bacon in the fridge. Cereal in the pantry. Feel free to browse."

She couldn't seem to stop the flow of words. Too many. Too fast. Almost certainly too revealing.

"I'm fine." His eyes fell again to the papers before he looked up to smile at her. "I'll clean up before I leave. Like the bed corners, it's a habit."

She couldn't remember ever having seen him smile. Whatever had stirred in her chest a moment ago happened again, but lower this time.

And that was *not* surprise, she acknowledged. Not deep in the bottom of her stomach.

"It doesn't matter. Call me if you find something." She tilted her head toward the stacks of material.

"Like I said. You'll be the first to know."

She didn't want to leave. She wanted to sit down in the chair beside him and read whatever he was reading. Talk about it. Talk to him. Instead...

"I have to go."

"I know. Good luck with the jackals."

She nodded, and then forced herself to turn and walk toward the door to the living room. When she reached it, she couldn't resist looking back at him.

Head down, he'd already returned to his perusal of the opened files. The morning sun picked out blue highlights in the darkness of his hair.

What was she doing? Mooning like a teenager over a man who...

Who was what? Crazy? Damaged?

Brain-damaged, she amended. Whatever the hell that meant.

Jake Underwood seemed more normal than most of

the people she knew. Certainly more normal than she was right now.

Taking a deep breath, she opened the front door and stepped out on the wide veranda that ran along the front and down one side of her house. In spite of the shade it provided, and the fact that it was only a little after eight in the morning, the heat struck her like a physical blow. And despite it, she was expected to be cool, calm and collected for the horde of reporters who would be waiting at the courthouse.

Jackals. Her lips tilted. A damned apt description from someone whose brain was supposed to be screwed up.

She managed to hang on to that smile most of the way downtown, losing it only to the reality of how appropriate Jake's description truly was.

DEALING WITH THE PRESS hadn't been the worst part of Eden's day, but it was certainly near the top for that honor. Since Jake's seemingly psychic description of the bunker they'd found was now well-known, most of the questions had revolved around his possible role in the kidnapping. Other than reiterating the things she'd been saying since his flashbacks concerning Raine had become public knowledge, there wasn't much she could do to defuse the town's growing hysteria.

And when the father of the kidnapped child became one of the more vocal critics of law enforcement's efforts to direct the investigation along avenues they believed would be more productive, the media became exactly what Jake had called them.

Although she wasn't particularly hopeful, Eden had found herself wondering, during the almost frenetic activities of the day, whether he'd discovered anything in her father's files that might be helpful. Because if he hadn't…

She felt again the even heavier weight of responsibility she bore for finding Raine. She'd been wrong about the bunker keeping the agents in town. If anything, the fact that it had been found—and found empty—seemed to solidify their decision to leave.

She had been assured they would be available for consultation; but she could see in their eyes that as far as they were concerned, the outcome of this case had been decided. The child they had come here to find was dead. If at some future date the department located her body, that would provide closure for the family and the possibility of forensic evidence that might lead to her killer. If that occurred, they had urged her to place a call to Jackson, and they'd get an evidence team right down here.

Which meant that, from now on, the Waverly police were virtually on their own. And other than continuing to do what they were currently doing, Eden had no idea where to go from here.

"I'm going home."

She looked up to find Dean leaning into the open door of her office. "Get some sleep," she urged. "And something to eat."

"You do the same." He had already turned when her question stopped him.

"What do we tell them tomorrow?"

"The Nolans?"

"The search teams." The number of people who had shown up for those had decreased with each passing day. And now they were searching areas they'd been over before.

"The same thing we've told them every day. Our best chance of finding her is to have everybody out looking."

"You think he took her out on the water?"

Dean shrugged as if it didn't matter. "That's always been a possibility."

"We may never know what happened to her."

"We *know* what happened to her, Eden. We may never find her body, but we all know what happened."

She nodded, too dispirited to argue with the reality of that. A reality she knew better than most.

Winton stuck his head in the door, looking from one to the other. "Am I interrupting something?"

"I was just leaving," Dean said.

"Major Underwood's here to see you, Chief."

Although she noted Dean's brows lift, Eden instructed, "Send him back."

When the deputy disappeared down the hall, Dean said, "Given the mood of this town, the man's either exceptionally brave or a fool."

"I don't think he's a fool."

"So I heard."

The undertone was impossible to miss. Or ignore. "What does that mean?"

"Somebody mentioned his truck was parked in front of your place all night."

"And?" Despite the calmness of her response, her heart had begun to pound.

"You being intimate with Underwood makes your defense of him a whole lot less believable to folks around here."

"My being *intimate* with him? Where the hell did you get that idea?"

"Why, I don't know, Eden. Maybe from him spending the night at your house."

She thought about telling Dean exactly why Jake had stayed. Although intimacy had nothing to do with it, the real reason would only make her look weak. Something she'd rather avoid before a subordinate, particularly in the current situation.

As she tried to think of some plausible explanation for Jake spending the night, she heard Winton direct him down the hall to her office. "We can talk about this tomorrow," she suggested instead.

"Whatever you say, Chief." Dean's tone was as mocking as it had been when he'd thrown his bombshell.

And it was the first time she could remember him addressing her with anything other than respect.

"Major Underwood." Dean nodded as he walked by Jake and out into the reception area.

"Your deputy said to come on back," Jake apologized.

"It's fine. We were just touching base about tomorrow." Eden could feel the rush of blood to her cheeks. As she'd told Dean, Jake was no fool.

"Rough day?" He hadn't yet stepped inside the office, as if unsure of his welcome.

"The Bureau pulled out."

"Can they do that?"

"Essentially, they said to call them when we find the body. Actually, it was more like *if* we find the body."

"They're playing the odds. They knew from the first that would be the most likely outcome."

"If giving up is playing the odds, then what are we doing?"

"Assuming she's alive. *Until* we have proof to the contrary."

"I'm not sure I can do that anymore." After today, hope was in very short supply.

"Then you need to turn the investigation over to someone who can."

"If I knew who that might be, I would."

"You give up now, Eden, she'll never be found."

"Then give me something to work with."

She had meant that to be theoretical. Or maybe she was hoping, as she had for the past three days, that Jake would have another of those flashbacks in which he saw Raine.

Whatever she had meant, his response caught her off guard. Jake limped across the room to place something on her desk.

Her recognition was instantaneous—file folders from her

father's cardboard box. She looked up from them and straight into Jake's eyes.

There was no sense of "gotcha" there. No promise. And no hype.

Apparently, he was giving her exactly what she had asked for. Something to work with.

Chapter Fifteen

"There are two that have some striking similarities to this kidnapping." Jake spread the folders out, although he knew the names at the top by heart. "Shauna Terrell in Boothville, Louisiana, 1999, and Madison Stewart, 2005, in Bayou La Batre, Alabama."

"What kind of similarities?" Eden's question seemed careful.

Maybe she simply didn't want to get her hopes up before she had something concrete to pin them on. Jake thought he could give her that.

"In both cases the kidnapper used an underground dugout to conceal his victim. More important, in both instances the hiding place had been constructed on either public or corporate land."

There was no reaction in her eyes. At least not the one he'd anticipated. She seemed underwhelmed by the connection he'd found so obvious between the three disappearances.

"But...wouldn't that make sense?" she asked finally. "If he did that, then even if someone discovered the dugout, there would be no way to tie it to him."

"Except a perpetrator of this kind of act isn't usually motivated by what makes sense. In most of these crimes, the kidnapper wants to keep his victim as close to him as possible. In his basement. Attic. Somewhere he can be with her.

These three—" he again touched the folders on her desk. "They didn't have that proximity. And that argues he has more control than most of those who commit these offenses."

"Three?"

"I'm including Raine's kidnapper."

"So you think this is someone who lived in Alabama and Louisiana before he came here?"

He had known she would find that a stretch. That some criminal newcomer to Waverly, where everyone knew everyone else's business, could escape detection. "Or someone who knew those areas. Maybe he hunted or fished there."

Her laugh was disbelieving. "We don't have to go out of state to hunt and fish."

"Then maybe he was visiting family in those locations and encountered the victims. Or maybe he moved here after the last of them. Maybe he had family here. Or grew up here and came back home."

"That's possible," she admitted. "A lot of people feel the grass is greener somewhere else. Or they just get tired of the confinement of small-town life."

"So you think this is worth pursuing?"

"I'll have to look at the files. But if the bunker is the only thing they have in common—" She looked up, her eyes apologetic.

"It's not. Looking at these places on the map, the towns where these abductions took place seem tellingly similar to me. You're probably more familiar with all the things they have in common than I am. Coastal waterways for one. A lot of the population involved in activities that depend on those waters. And a lot of uninhabited land."

"What about the kidnapping themselves?"

Jake had known that would be the part he'd have the most difficulty convincing her about. His own conviction was so strong, however, that he was determined to make her see what he had seen.

"One of these was a home invasion, much like Raine's. The girl was taken from her bed in the middle of the night. The rest of the family slept through the entire thing."

"And the other?"

"The child was playing outside after dark. Or almost dark. She disappeared from the family's front yard."

"Then how can you make a connection?"

"Because of the bunker. And the physical similarities." He opened one of the folders and pulled out the picture of the girl who had disappeared in Alabama. "Look at her."

"Oh, my God," Eden breathed softly. "She and Raine—"

"Could be sisters."

Jake regretted the words as soon as they came out of his mouth, but Eden didn't react, her eyes still on the picture. And as he'd presented the evidence he'd found, his own confidence in it had grown.

There were too many things that pointed to this being the same perpetrator. A conclusion he might never have reached had Eden's father not laid the groundwork.

"I don't know a lot about the psychology of this kind of crime, but don't serial killers seek out victims of the same physical type?" he prompted.

"We need to run this by the FBI." She was still studying the picture.

"You mean the guys who have given Raine up as dead?"

She looked up at that. "Even if they have, they haven't given up finding her killer."

"You turn this over to them to pursue, how long will that take?"

"What do you want me to do, Jake?"

"Think about who in Waverly might fit this profile. Who has moved here from one of these two locations? Or who has family living in one of them? *Use* the fact that this is the kind of place where you know all about your neighbor to your advantage." He touched the folders on her desk. "And find him before he does to Raine what he did to these two little girls."

"What was that?" she asked, holding his eyes.

"He killed them," he said bluntly.

"How long?"

The pertinent question. As far as their chances of rescuing Raine were concerned.

With his forefinger, he pushed the folder containing the details of the Louisiana case toward her. "Her body was too decomposed to tell when it was found."

"And this one?" Eden held out the picture of the girl who'd been taken in Alabama.

The blonde child who looked enough like the picture he'd found in the file marked Christie to be *her* sister, as well.

"The investigators on that case believe he kept her alive for at least four days. The coroner couldn't be any more precise than that."

He watched the impact in her eyes. Four days. A time frame they had passed yesterday.

JAKE HAD LEFT the files and the notes he'd taken on them for her to study. Even with the day's almost constant interruptions, Eden had finally managed to read through all of it.

In spite of her initial skepticism, there were undeniable elements in the other two cases that mirrored the kidnapping of the Nolans' daughter. Jake's premise was worth investigating. Especially, she reminded herself, when she had nothing else.

She automatically glanced at the clock as she reached for the phone. Her hand hesitated in midair when she saw how late it was.

Dean would be asleep. And although he would be the ideal person to pose Jake's questions to, she couldn't in good conscience wake him for information that half a hundred other people in town could just as easily provide.

She pushed up from her desk, stretching muscles cramped from too many hours spent hunched in the same position. Then she walked down the hall toward the common area of the station, her footsteps echoing off the narrow walls.

Winton was manning the front desk. He might be young, but he had been born here. His family, like Jake's, had been founders of the community.

"Going home?" he asked, looking up from whatever he was reading.

"Not yet. Who else is around?"

Winton considered her question before he shook his head. "I think we're it. Everybody's pretty much worn out."

That was nothing less than the truth, Eden acknowledged. Everyone in the department had worked overtime on this, and most of that hadn't been on the clock.

"You know anybody in town who has Alabama roots?" Considering how quickly the information about Jake's flash-backs had become public knowledge, she didn't want to make this new avenue of investigation grist for the gossip mill. But she didn't really believe Winton was the source of that leak. If she had, she would never have broached this subject with him.

"The Carmichaels. I think their family was originally from Montgomery. 'Course, I guess that was a pretty long time ago."

Edna and Sam Carmichael were in their eighties. "Anybody else you can think of?"

"Wasn't Miz Greene originally from Dothan?"

Lincoln Greene's wife, Laurie. Lincoln Greene, whose pickup had been parked at the end of Jake's drive the night someone had taken potshots at her.

"Are you sure?"

"Not really," the kid said with a grin. "My mom would know. She remembers that kind of stuff. You want me to call her?"

Eden believed that if she told Winton her inquiry was to

be kept confidential, he would respect her request. She wasn't sure that his mother would.

"Thanks, but it's not that important. Oh, and don't mention to anyone that I was asking about this. You know how people take anything and run with it these days."

"You don't want to make trouble for Miz Greene," Winton said. "I get it."

"Thanks. You here all night?"

"Only till midnight. Then Carl comes in."

"Okay. I'm going to call it a day. Don't hesitate to wake me if something comes up."

"Will do. Want me to look at the county records?"

Puzzled, Eden turned back to him. "For…?"

"The Alabama thing you asked about."

"What would you check?"

"I don't know. I was thinking driver's licenses. Don't you have to submit your old one to get a replacement?"

"I'm not sure. The state handles those."

"I can look into it if you want. I'm not doing much good just sitting here."

"Then why not?" she asked with a smile. "See you in the morning."

"Get some rest."

"You, too."

"I'll sleep in tomorrow. I need to catch up on some of that stuff. Like everybody else, I guess," the deputy said almost apologetically.

Eden nodded agreement and continued to the outer door.

Playing catch-up was exactly what the department was doing. On sleep and everything else. After the frantic activity of the first few days, the search for Raine had become routine, and once more, eating and sleeping had taken precedence over searching and strategizing.

Although she felt guilty about that, that initial frenzy had gotten them no closer to the child than they were now. And other than Jake's idea that this kidnapping might be connected to the ones he'd discovered in her father's materials, there was nothing new to pursue.

In light of that, she changed her previous decision and pulled out her cell. As she climbed into the cruiser, she punched up Dean's number. If she woke him, as tired as they all were, she had no doubt he would be able to go back to sleep.

"'Lo."

Not asleep, Eden thought in relief. "I need to run something by you."

"Okay."

"There are a couple of child abductions, one in Boothville, Louisiana, and another in Bayou La Batre, that bear some striking similarities to Raine's. Can you think of anyone in town who has connections to either of those locations?"

"What kind of similarities?" Dean sounded more confused than excited.

"Use of a bunker located on public land. Similar demographics of the areas. Victimology. One of the girls looks enough like Raine that they could be sisters. Home invasion."

"Are you saying you think they were all committed by the same kidnapper?"

"I'm saying it right now, that seems like a possibility. Look, I don't know that this will lead to anything, but I think it's worth checking out. Can you think of anybody who might have lived in either place?"

The silence on the other end was prolonged. When Dean broke it, there was a trace of irritation in his tone. "Not right now. Where are you?"

"Leaving the office. Did I wake you?"

"Yeah. I'll think about it when I'm more functional."

"Okay. Sorry. I just thought it was something we should look into."

"The Bureau call you?"

"About this? No." She hesitated, reluctant to admit it had been Jake's idea. Reluctant also for some reason—maybe nothing more than her father's secretiveness—to reveal the source of Jake's inspiration. "This came from somewhere else. It may not amount to anything, but...I don't know what else to do."

"Sometimes there *isn't* anything else, Eden."

"Yeah, well, I'm not to the point of admitting that. Go back to sleep. If somebody comes to mind, give me a call."

"Tonight?"

"Of course. If you think of something."

"I'm not much for thinking when I'm asleep."

Eden wished she could say the same. Raine haunted her dreams as well as her waking hours. "Just call me if you do. Okay?"

"Whatever you say, Chief."

The click on the other end seemed abrupt. As did Dean's closing comment.

She laid her phone on the seat beside her, trying to chalk both up as the result of too little sleep and too much frustration. After all, the agents had never once suggested that this case followed a pattern established in any previous kidnappings. And she had to admit, despite being personally willing to grasp at straws, the connections Jake had found were tenuous.

Based on what she had right now, she didn't feel justified in waking anyone else. In the morning she'd contact Doc Murphy, who not only knew everyone in town, but also had an encyclopedic memory. She would also check out Winton's comment about Laurie Greene. And, given Dean's reaction, she would also call the FBI to get their take on the other two cases.

The rest of tonight she would try to sleep without allowing the images of what might be happening to Raine as she did invade her dreams. Unlike Jake's flashbacks, she had no faith in her nightmares indicating anything other than a sense of desperation.

SINCE SHE'D EXPECTED to be home well before midnight, she hadn't left any lights on in the house. Not only was the darkness uninviting, so was the obvious emptiness of the rooms she passed through. And although the cardboard box in which her father had kept his files was still on the kitchen table, the man who had spent the night guarding her was gone.

She filled a glass from the dispenser on the refrigerator door and downed a couple of the ibuprofen p.m. tablets Jake had given her to help her sleep. Then she carried the water with her into the bathroom, setting it down on the counter as she started to unbutton her shirt.

She was still thinking about people who might fit Jake's profile when her eyes lifted to the mirror above the sink. The words, written in what looked like blood, seemed to leap off the glass.

Christie says come out and play.

She took a step back as if to escape their impact, but as with the quilt and the doll, there was no escape. Whoever was doing this knew too much about her sister's kidnapping. And exactly how to taunt her with its outcome.

Was that the intent? To convince her that she would have no more success finding Raine than the police had had in locating Christie? Or was it possible that there was some real connection between this missing child and the long-ago disappearance of her sister?

A door slammed at the back of the house, breaking through her shocked paralysis. Without thinking of the possible consequences, she whirled and ran toward the sound.

She had switched off the light when she'd left the kitchen. In the darkness moonlight spilled across the tile floor from the glass of the back door. The security chain, which she never unfastened except to take out the garbage once a week, swung gently back and forth.

Whoever had written that message on the mirror had been inside the house when she'd arrived. And he had wanted her to know that.

Infuriated rather than frightened, she crossed the room to turn the lock and secure the chain. As she did, she looked out into the yard. Nothing moved, the shadows thick under the trees and along the side of the garage.

Her weapon was still in her utility belt, which, from force of habit, she had draped over the back of the couch. She retrieved the Glock, its familiar feel reassuring.

She lifted the edge of the front drapes to peer out into the street. In the spill of dappled light under the sheltering oaks, the neighborhood was as peaceful as the backyard had been.

Her every instinct urged her to go outside. To find the bastard who was trying to terrorize her and put an end to this once and for all.

Her training dictated that she call for backup instead. To stay inside until whoever the dispatcher sent out arrived and conducted a thorough search of the grounds. By then, of course, she knew the intruder would be long gone.

Somehow, he had access to her house. He'd been inside it at least twice, despite her increased vigilance in locking her windows and doors. And, unless she wanted to give up sleeping here, there was apparently no way to prevent him from coming in again.

So instead of calling the dispatcher, she turned the dead bolt on the front door and eased out into the shadows cast by the overhang of the wide veranda.

Ready or not, you bastard, I'm coming after you.

Chapter Sixteen

Jake had expected her to call. To tell him that the FBI had denied the connections he thought he'd seen. Or that she didn't think they were strong enough to waste the department's limited manpower in pursuing. To tell him *something*. That she hadn't bothered to contact him at all was, he supposed, as telling as putting her doubts into words.

Despite the hours he'd spent reading her father's files last night, sleep eluded him. Thoughts and theories ricocheted uncontrollably through his head until he'd given up and crawled out of the sweat-tangled sheets.

He stood now in his grandmother's kitchen, looking out at the moonlight filtering through the branches of moss-draped oaks. For some reason, his nerves were as taut as they had always been before the start of a mission.

There was nothing in the quiet darkness to produce that anxiety. Nothing that should make his hands tremble or his heart race.

He closed his fingers tightly over the rolled edge of the old-fashioned sink, willing them to stillness. At the same time he leaned forward, breathing through his mouth. Something was wrong. Something—

The shadows he watched danced suddenly, evolving into shapes as familiar to him now as the planes of his own face. The transport directly in front of theirs, silhouetted against the distant mountains. Silhouetted until it dissolved into a plume of flame and black smoke.

He smelled the fire first. And then the rest, rushing into his consciousness like a flood. Blood and heated metal and burning gasoline. Underlying all of them was the undeniable stench of death.

The sounds followed. Tearing at him. Shredding his control as they always did.

Suddenly, unexpectedly, the desert brightness spun away, leaving an unfamiliar darkness in its place. And in the stillness that was left when the cursing and screaming had stopped was the sound of someone crying.

Soft. Hopeless. Lost.

Then that, too, was gone, leaving the quiet moonlight to paint his grandmother's neglected flowerbeds with a beauty they had not possessed since her death.

He took a breath, aware once more of the grip his fingers had found over the porcelain. He forced them to loosen and made himself breathe again.

There was no doubt in his mind about what he had heard. Someone crying. And not the harsh sobbing noises Martinez had made as he died.

Although he hadn't seen her, he knew who cried in that darkness. And he also knew that this time the sounds she made had been born not of terror, but despair.

THE FAMILIAR HAD become foreign in the moonlight. And Eden had no idea what direction the man she sought had taken.

Avoiding the antique wicker furniture on the porch, she edged along the front of the house, the Glock, held with both hands, leading the way. She reached the corner of the house, her spine still pressed against the wall. She took a breath and then turned her head sharply to scan the backyard. Nothing disturbed the expanse of lawn that eventually gave way to the grasses that grew along the finger of the inlet that backed this neighborhood.

It had been at least three minutes since the slamming of the kitchen door. Whoever had been inside her house could be anywhere by now.

Alert for any movement, she turned the corner and took a careful step forward. As she moved, her gaze swung back and forth from her own backyard to the Perrys' home on her right.

By now her eyes had adjusted to the lack of light. The shadows under the trees were heavy, but there was no darker anomaly among them. Once more, her gaze lifted to the inlet.

Using a rowboat would have lessened the chances of the intruder being seen. Anyone who knew the area well would be able to navigate out there, even at night. Especially as bright...

The mental image was sudden: a full moon casting a swath of light across the smooth black surface of the water. Illuminating every cypress knee and black-gum stump in its path.

She began to run, zigzagging, as she had watched Jake do only a few nights ago, in order to take advantage of the concealment afforded by the patches of shadow.

How long had it been now? Five minutes? Six? Long enough for him to have paddled out of the slough and into the inlet itself?

She reached the edge of the cordgrass, her breath rasping in and out. The pier her father had built stretched into the water like a reaching finger. Her feet pounded across its wooden boards as her eyes searched the surface of the slough.

The wide trail of moonlight lay across its smooth darkness, just as she had pictured it. But there was no boat. And no boatman.

Why would there be? she realized. If he wanted to escape detection, especially if he were a local, he would be skirting the banks. Hiding in the area where the low-growing vegetation of the land merged seamlessly with the marsh grasses of the water.

It was too dark there to identify any shape as a vessel. She held her breath instead, listening for the unmistakable plop and stroke of a paddle.

The gentle lap of the water against the pilings beneath her and the familiar nighttime chorus of insects masked any sound he might make. She had begun to turn back toward the house, when a movement along the far bank caught her eye.

She whirled and raised her weapon. She deliberately held her breath as her finger tightened over the trigger in anticipation.

Slowly, a blue heron emerged from the shadows, majestic wings spread to lift it into the ribbon of moonlight. Unthinkingly, she followed the trajectory of the bird's flight with the Glock until she realized what she was doing. She lowered the gun, releasing the breath she had held to steady her aim.

Bastard. You damn bastard.

She drew air into her aching lungs, the sound like a sob. The pent-up frustrations of the past week screamed for release, but she denied them. If he were out there in the darkness, she wouldn't give him the satisfaction of knowing he had made her cry.

She caught her breath again, snubbing like a child on the edge of tears. She refused to shed them. She turned instead, moving carefully through the shadows toward the house.

Her home. And she swore that whoever he was, that bastard would never set foot inside it again.

JAKE SNAPPED HIS PHONE closed and laid it on the center console of his truck. He increased his speed, as once more he devoted his total concentration to the road.

Maybe Eden had taken something to help her sleep. Despite how logical the explanation was, he didn't believe it.

She wouldn't take anything that would knock her out so

completely she couldn't hear her phone. That would be so
out of character that, despite his growing fear, he couldn't
convince himself of the possibility.

He had thought about going by police headquarters,
but found himself turning instead onto the narrow side
street where he'd parked last night. The small, well-kept
houses, mostly postwar-era bungalows, were all dark, their
inhabitants sleeping in the cocooned isolation of their air-
conditioning systems.

The same instincts that had seen him through dozens of
missions caused him to kill his lights as he glided to a stop
more than a block from Eden's front door. He waited in the car
long enough to make a thorough survey of the empty street.

Nothing stirred around him. No porch lights came on. No
dogs barked.

Reaching up, he switched off the dome light and then
opened the door. He stepped out onto the sidewalk and using
whatever cover the suburban terrain afforded—the trunks of
the moss-draped oaks, the wild hydrangea and azalea bushes
and even the shadows cast by the cars parked along the curb—
made his way toward the house where he'd stood guard last
night.

Halfway there, he realized he'd left his cell on the console.
The decision not to go back was easily made, because by now
he could see that, among all the darkened houses on the street,
a light was burning in Eden's.

Something was wrong. He had known it from the first
time she'd failed to answer her phone. Had known it with the
same inexplicable connection he felt to the terrified child in
his flashbacks.

Hurrying now, he skirted the side of the house next to
hers, praying there was no dog in its fenced yard. He had
somehow escaped detection in the sleeping neighborhood,
but as he began to cross the open expanse between the two
bungalows, he knew how far he had pushed his luck.

Simultaneously with that thought, a figure appeared out of the shadows of Eden's bungalow to assume the classic shooter's stance in front of him. Feet slightly spread, knees bent, both hands locked around the weapon that was pointed at his midsection.

His recognition was instinctive. Almost instantaneous.

"Eden," he said softly. "It's me. It's Jake."

"What were you doing in my house?"

He examined the question, using the information it provided to piece together the scenario that had brought her out here. "Somebody was in your house?"

Another incident like the one with doll?

"Answer me, damn it," she demanded. "Was it you I heard inside?"

"I wouldn't do that. You *know* I wouldn't do that."

The gun she held didn't waver, but she seemed to be considering his denial. "Then why are you sneaking around out here in the dark?"

"I think she's alive."

Another silence, longer than the last. "Raine? You saw her?"

He was tempted, at least briefly, to say he had. The truth might be less compelling, but it was the truth. Eden deserved that.

"I heard her."

"Heard?"

"I heard her crying."

"But you didn't see her?"

"No," he admitted. And waited.

After a dozen heartbeats, she lowered the Glock and straightened. "Then how can you be sure it was her?"

"I don't know. I just am. I heard her."

"Crying." She repeated the word as if she found it unbelievable.

"She sounded... I don't know. Lost, maybe." That was it

exactly, he realized as he said the word. She had sounded lost
Alone.

But not as terrified as she had been before.

"I don't know what that means, Jake."

He shook his head. "All I know is that she's alive."

"Is she in the same place where you saw her before?"

"I don't know," he said again.

He knew how thin this all sounded. Why in the world
should she believe him? *He* wouldn't. Not if some nutcase
was telling him this crazy story.

"But you're sure what you heard was Raine?"

Was he? All he could be certain of now was that the crying
he'd heard tonight hadn't been Martinez.

"I thought I was. I thought it was her," he amended.

She shook her head. "I don't see how—"

"It happened just like before. Everything was the same a
it always is, and then it all… I don't know. Changed. Shifted
Became something else. Something that was taking plac
in the darkness. Somewhere damp. And I heard crying. I
wasn't any of the others. The men I was with that day. I know
the sounds they make." He should. He had heard them in a
hundred nightmares. "This was… I really think it was her
Eden. I'm sure of it."

"Okay. Okay. That's good. If it's her. That's good, isn't it
That means she's still alive."

The intake of breath that followed the last word wa
strange. Wrong. He knew it, just as he had known somethin
was wrong when he'd seen the light on in her house.

For the first time the thought that whoever had been insid
might have injured her occurred to him. He'd been so caugh
up in wanting to tell her about Raine, he hadn't followed u
on what she'd said.

"Are you okay? He didn't hurt you, did he?" Despite th
weapon she held, he approached her, putting both hands o
her shoulders.

She looked up at him, her eyes wide and dark. Her lips parted as if she intended to speak, but she shook her head instead. And then, in a move so unexpected it took his breath, she moved against him, burying her face against the center of his chest.

He waited a moment, unsure what the correct response to that should be. Remembering the endless warnings from the therapist the Army had required him to see about not over-reacting to situations. About always thinking before he did something. About the need to exert an ironclad control over his emotions.

Ignoring them all, he released Eden's shoulders, wrapping his arms around her as he gathered her to him. She turned her head to the side, her cheek over his heart. He could feel the Glock against his spine as her hands moved behind his back, to settle around his waist.

"It's okay." His lips moved over the fragrance of her hair as he whispered those words of comfort. "He's gone. It's over."

"I wanted to kill the bastard."

"A damned healthy response."

The sound of her laughter was muffled against his shirt. "You're probably the only person I know who would say that."

"I *have* been told I'm no longer a good arbitrator of what's appropriate."

She pushed away from him to once more look into his eyes. "Because of your injuries?"

His laugh was short. And bitter. "The politically correct term is 'brain trauma.' Not that I'm big on political correctness. I'm not crazy, Eden, I swear to you. Even the doctors haven't suggested that. And other than the change in the flashbacks, nothing has happened here to contradict their assessment."

"We're a pair, aren't we?"

Despite liking the sound of that, he wasn't sure what she was getting at. "I don't understand."

"I'm the one with the phantom. Someone who can come into my house whenever he wants. Despite locked doors and windows."

"He isn't a phantom." There were a few military terms he could use to describe the guy, but he was enjoying the sensation of holding her too much to risk scaring her off by using them.

"I know. What I don't know is how he found out about my sister. *Nobody* down here knew. My dad never talked about her, because he couldn't bear to. Neither of us did. So how can this bastard know everything about what happened to her?"

"The same way your father learned about all those other cases. All the kidnappings he investigated. The information's out there. It doesn't take a law-enforcement officer to track down that kind of stuff these days. All it takes is an internet connection."

"Do you think it's possible this could be the same person who took Raine? If so, then why would he do this? I was only a couple of minutes behind him tonight. If I'd been quicker, I might have seen him. Why expose himself to that kind of risk?"

"To distract you?" Jake suggested, although he didn't believe Raine's kidnapper was the one playing these mind games.

"But he *hasn't*. My entire focus since this started has been on finding Raine. The other… It's been a sideshow, I'll admit, but…" Her eyes begged him to believe her. "I never once lost sight of what's at stake."

"So where do we go from here?"

"Now that we know she's still alive," she said softly, "we go find Raine."

Chapter Seventeen

"Thanks, Doc. And again, I'm sorry to wake you in the middle of the night."

"Not the first time I've had a phone call at this hour, Eden. Don't you worry about it. And if I think of anybody, I'll call you."

"I owe you. Again."

The old man's chuckle was all the response she got to her expression of gratitude. That and his promise to call if he thought of someone in town who fit the description she'd laid out for him.

When she put down the phone, she looked up at Jake, who was standing at the side of her desk. She shook her head and read the disappointment, quickly hidden, in his eyes.

"Who's next?" he asked.

"Winton mentioned that his mom keeps up with family connections. We could call her."

"Winton?"

"The younger deputy that works the front desk."

"The guy there when we came in."

"Winton left at midnight." Eden glanced at her watch. "He should be home by now."

"You have his number?"

"I can get it." She punched the intercom button and waited

for the deputy up front to answer. "Carl, I need Winton's number. Preferably his cell if you have it. Home phone if not."

"That'll take a minute."

"I'll wait." She released the button and looked up at Jake again. "He was going to try and check the records of local driver's license applications. He didn't call me, so maybe he didn't find anything. Or maybe the license procedure doesn't work the way he thought it did."

"Or maybe you were out chasing phantoms when he tried to reach you. I couldn't get you, either."

"Chief."

In response to the deputy's voice, Eden pressed the intercom again. "Okay."

"This is his cell. And I've got the home number, if you want that."

"Give me both." She wrote down the numbers as the deputy called them out. "Thanks, Carl."

"And, Chief?"

"Yes?"

"Winton and I talked this all out before he left. If Major Underwood is here about filing those charges the chief deputy mentioned, then I'm real sorry. We only did what he told us to."

"I don't understand."

"We let Dave go. It was after midnight. He said if the major hadn't come in by the end of the day, we had to release him."

Eden raised her brows in question to Jake, who shook his head.

"That's okay, Carl. You did the right thing. Major Underwood decided not to press charges."

"Good. I mean I'm glad we didn't screw up. When I saw him come in with you, I was afraid that's what he was here for."

"No, it's okay. Thanks for the numbers." She released the

button. "I don't know why Porter was still here. I would have thought he'd have made bond."

"Maybe he didn't have the money."

"Then I guess we should pay him more."

"He works for the department?"

"He's a mechanic. He keeps our cars running, and we certainly can't afford to replace them. Nobody else can touch what he charges us."

"No family to raise the bail for him?"

She shook her head as she picked up the phone and began punching in the number of Winton's cell. It rang several times before the deputy answered.

"Hello?"

"Sorry to wake you," Eden said. "I need you to do what we talked about before?"

"Ma'am?"

"I need you to ask your mom about some people in town. About their family connections."

"She's asleep. You want me to go wake her up?"

"I do, Winton. I'm sorry, but I think this is that important."

"Okay. Let me get her, and I'll call you back."

"As soon as you can." Eden thought about telling him this concerned the Nolan kidnapping, but in spite of having bought into Jake's certainty to this point, she found she wasn't quite ready to share his theory with the world.

As she put the phone down, there was a knock on her door. "Come in."

With his elbow, Carl pushed the opening wide enough to peer in. "I thought y'all might want some coffee. I just made it, so it's fresh."

She glanced at Jake, who nodded. "Thanks, Carl."

Jake took the mugs from the deputy's hand, putting one of them down in front of her.

"I didn't want y'all to try to drink the stuff left in the pot. Not fit for man or beast."

Jake raised the mug he held, taking a long swallow. "This is great."

"Thanks. And thanks for not pressing charges against Dave. I know he goes off half-cocked sometimes, but he's a good guy. He's taught me a lot about cars and engines."

Jake nodded again, avoiding the necessity of commenting on Porter's character by taking another sip of coffee.

"They say you did a number on him," the deputy said admiringly. "That ol' coon ass claims to have come up the hard way, but I guess that don't make him a match for somebody from the Special Forces."

That ol' coon ass. Eden replayed the sentence in her head to make sure the words had been in reference to Porter.

"What did you just say?" she demanded.

"Sorry, Chief. I didn't mean any disrespect." Carl cut his eyes toward Jake, as if to establish some sort of male bond between the two of them.

"Did you just call Porter a coon ass?"

"I'm really sorry, Chief, but Dave says it himself all the time. It's not something bad. Not like—" He stopped, his eyes again seeking approval or support from Jake.

"Dave Porter's from Louisiana," Eden said aloud. There was no other explanation for what Carl had just said. And as she made that realization, the others followed.

"That's why she's alone," she said to Jake. "We've had him in jail for the past two days. She *is* alone. She has been since—"

She stopped because she had come to the final, terrible realization. "We let him go. We let him leave, so he can go back to her. Oh, my God, Jake, he's on his way back to her right now."

EDEN WAS BEGINNING to regret her decision to do this by the book. Her first instinct had been to rush out to Porter's by herself and find Raine. To get her away from him as fast as she could.

But if she wasn't successful in doing that, it would give Porter a chance to get away, possibly taking the child with him. Or even worse, allow him to put an end to this kidnapping in the same way those other two cases had ended.

She had notified Dean first, not only because he was in the closest physical proximity to the office, but also because he was the most experienced officer on the force. Although her chief deputy had arrived at the station within five minutes of her call, his reaction to Carl's revelation was turning out to be less than supportive.

"Have you lost your ever-loving mind?" he asked, when she explained her decision. "You can't go out there with guns blazing on something as flimsy as this."

Eden raised her eyes from the shotgun she was loading. "Major Underwood is pressing assault charges against David Porter. I'm going out there to arrest him."

"You're going out there because the two of you think he's the one who took Raine."

"Yes." She shoved the second cartridge in the riot gun.

"Based on a bunch of crap he came up with." Dean pointed a shaking finger at Jake, who had so far held his peace.

"Based on the similarities of this case and the one in Boothville."

"Hell, you don't even know if Porter's ever been there. You don't know *where* in Louisiana he's from. All you know is that Carl Youngblood called him a coon ass. Been called that myself a time or two. And I ain't from Louisiana."

"If you add that to the similarities in the cases—"

"Yeah, two little girls were abducted. One from her bed and one from her front yard." The sarcasm was thick. "That's real concrete evidence they're connected right there."

"Two little girls who look alike."

"*All* little girls that age look alike."

"I'm going out there to make an arrest for assault." Eden worked on keeping her tone reasoned, but she couldn't resist snapping the barrel of the weapon closed. "We'll figure the rest out after that."

"You've lost your mind, Eden. You know that, don't you? You've let some brain-damaged pretty boy convince you that Dave Porter, somebody you've known for years, has made a practice of snatching and killing children."

Eden glanced at Jake to gauge his reaction to the term, but his face reflected none of the anger she felt on his behalf. He looked as relaxed as if she and Dean were discussing the weather.

"Nobody's convinced me of anything. I see enough similarities in these cases to bring the man in for questioning."

"Well, I don't believe it. I can tell you that."

"Are you going with me?"

"Not on your life."

She stabbed the intercom button. "Carl, I want you to call in Gibbons and Blake. Tell them to meet me at the intersection of Pugh Drive and County Road 79 in twenty minutes." It would take her at least that long to get out there.

"Yes, ma'am." The disembodied voice sounded shaken.

"And no sirens. You understand?" She didn't wait for an answer as she rounded the desk, the shotgun held across her body.

"You run this all by the FBI?" Dean demanded.

"An arrest for assault? I don't think they'd be interested."

"You trying to grab the glory in finding Raine all for yourself?"

She stopped, looking back at him. "I thought you didn't believe there was anything to this."

"I don't. But it's pretty clear *he's* convinced you there is. I'm thinking that after screwing around with this for a week, you're trying to make folks think you know what you're doing."

She laughed. "I *do* know what I'm doing. And I'd like your help to do it, Dean." She would, if for no other reason than that there was an element in town who had always believed she had been given this job because of who her father was, rather than because she deserved it. "We haven't created this out of whole cloth. It fits."

"You've lost your mind," he said again.

"Okay, but I'm still going to arrest Porter."

"We let him go, Eden. Told him it was over. The major there didn't do what we asked him to do—"

"And now he's changed his mind."

"What mind?" Dean muttered.

"I'll wait outside." Jake brushed by her as he walked to the door.

When it closed behind him, Eden turned back to her deputy. "What happened to all that you said at the beginning of this? About all the respect you had for his service to his country?"

"I respect his service. And I think he paid a damned heavy price for it. But I'm not going to pin my reputation and the reputation of this department on his say-so."

"Neither am I. But I *am* going to try and rescue a little girl who I believe Dave Porter abducted and is hiding out at his place."

"She's gone, Eden. Much as you and I would like to believe otherwise. The agents told you that before they left."

"If she is, then I'll have wasted some gas and some manpower tonight. And if she isn't..." She looked at him, hoping that he would respond to that possibility.

She could read nothing in his eyes but contempt. After a moment she turned on her heel and left Dean alone in the office he had apparently always believed should be his.

THE MOONLIGHT THAT had gilded his grandmother's rose garden mercilessly revealed the squalor that surrounded Dave Porter's house and its adjacent shop. Between the hulks of rusting cars and scattered engine parts, empty oil cans and broken bottles gleamed among the overgrown weeds.

They had parked the squad cars at the bottom of the rise leading up to the Porter homestead, which was located at the end of a long dirt road. Eden had led the way up the hill, followed by her two deputies.

Jake had brought up the rear, every sense alert to the possibility of an ambush. There seemed no way Porter could have warning of their approach, but his training to expect the unexpected was too ingrained to ignore.

The house they stood looking down on was dark, as was the outbuilding, topped by a fading sign that read Porter's Auto Repair and Service. The clearing on which the two buildings stood was surrounded by a thick pine forest. Large enough, Jake judged, with a sinking feeling in his stomach, to hide a battalion.

He knew from the explanation she'd given the two deputies that Eden had intended to knock on the front door and make the arrest, just as if they had no other reason for being out here. Everything after that depended on how Porter reacted.

Before he'd gotten into the cruiser with Eden, he'd retrieved his Kimber 1911 from the glove compartment of his truck. Although he had seen the deputies look at one another when he'd gotten out of the patrol car to accompany them to the top of the rise, neither had openly questioned his right to be there.

"If he's asleep," the deputy Eden had introduced as Billy Gibbons whispered, "we could kick down the door and take him before he's had a chance to get good awake."

"What would you do, Billy, if somebody kicked down your door in the middle of the night?" Her eyes remained on the buildings below.

"Shoot first and ask questions later," the other deputy, Marty Blake, supplied. "Anybody would."

"I'm not looking to get somebody shot," Eden said. "We're here to arrest a man for simple assault."

"I don't think he's down there," Gibbons said.

Eden turned to him then, eyes questioning.

"Dave drives that black, souped-up Z. You see it anywhere down there?"

There was a brief silence as they visually searched the compound below.

"He could be anywhere."

Jake read the despair in Eden's voice. She had hoped, as he had, that this would be the end of it. One way or another.

"He moved her," he reminded her. "Something that wasn't without risk. He did that because he wants her closer to him. Wherever he's keeping her, it's not far from here."

"Even if it's close, how do we find her? Look out there."

As Jake considered the wilderness that surrounded the place, he felt the same sense of hopelessness her voice had revealed. If only he'd done what she'd asked him to do, Porter would still be the Waverly jail. Instead...

"We start by searching the house and the grounds for anything that might tell us where he's hiding her. Who knows? Maybe we'll get lucky."

EDEN HAD TAKEN Billy Gibbons to the house, where she intended to follow through on their original plan. She would knock on the door. If there was no answer, they'd break it down and search the premises for anything that might indicate where Raine was being held.

There had been some argument from Blake, who she'd assigned to search the shop with Jake, about the fact that they didn't have a warrant, which would compromise any evidence they might find. Although Jake hadn't taken part in the discussion, the final consensus seemed to be that their first priority had to be finding the child. If they did that, then they'd worry about proving Porter's guilt later.

The moon seemed less bright as he and the deputy approached the outbuilding. Although both had drawn their weapons, Jake's anxiety was centered on Eden, who was far more likely to encounter Porter in the main house than they were out here. He had wanted to protest her decision to split them up, but had resisted because he didn't want to undermine her authority in front of her men.

The deputy he'd been assigned motioned him to the other side of the double doors, which stood slightly ajar. When Jake was in place, the other man placed his hand on the door nearest him. He mouthed the word, "Ready?"

At Jake's nod, Blake flung the door open and stepped inside, his weapon leveled at the interior. As Jake moved in behind him, they waited for their eyes to adjust to the increased darkness inside the building.

The smells of the shop drifted out into the night air. Gas and oil primarily, underlaid by mold and rot. Shards of moonlight knifed through hundreds of cracks and broken places in the rough wooden walls. Even in that dim illumination, it was clear the shop was empty.

"We need to check for a basement. Something underground," Jake whispered to his companion.

The deputy nodded, using the muzzle of his firearm to motion Jake to the far side of the garage. Working toward the middle of the cavernous space, they began checking the oil-stained boards.

"Hey," Blake whispered.

Jake turned, expecting him to be examining a suspicious configuration of the floor. Instead he was looking up at the automobile that was suspended above his head on the hydraulic rack. "What kind of car was it Billy said Porter drives?"

EDEN HAD HELD Billy back as long as she could, but when the minutes stretched with no response from inside the house, she nodded at him. The burly deputy put his shoulder against the front door, using his considerable strength to break its lock. He stepped inside immediately, leaving her to follow him into the darkness.

As her eyes adjusted, she saw Billy, his weapon leading the way, was checking out the living room. Before he'd secured the area, a scrambling noise from the kitchen sent him rushing in that direction. A shotgun blast, visible in the darkness, cut him down in midstride.

As Billy fell forward onto the linoleum floor, Eden took advantage of the protection offered by the door frame. She immediately turned her head to speak into her shoulder radio. "Officer down out at Dave Porter's house. We need reinforcements and paramedics here now."

Without waiting for the dispatcher's response, she inched forward until she could see into the moonlit kitchen. No further sound had emanated from the room after Billy's body hit the floor.

Eden told herself there was nothing she could do for her deputy now, but as she'd watched the blood spread like black ink across the pale floor, she knew she had to try.

She eased forward in a low squat, her Glock sweeping the area around her. The room was empty. Whoever had brought Billy down was no longer there.

As her fingers found the carotid artery at the side of the deputy's neck, her eyes continued to scan her surroundings. To her right was a door she assumed led outside. To the left—

The blow to the back of her skull seemed to destroy her ability to think. At least about anything other than the agony it had caused.

Somehow, despite its paralyzing force, she managed to hold on to consciousness. She tumbled forward, unable to get her hands up in time to prevent her sprawl across Billy's body.

As she fell, she lost her hold on the Glock. Almost detached from the implications of what was happening, she watched as it skittered away into the shadows.

The fingers that fastened over her upper arms bit hard into her flesh, as the man who had circled around behind her to deliver that devastating blow pulled her roughly to her feet. She struggled to keep the encroaching fog of unconsciousness at bay as he dragged her toward the door she'd noticed on the right.

As they went through it, she tried to grab at the frame, only to be struck savagely once more, this time on her temple. And then, at last, everything faded to blackness.

As SOON AS HE'D identified the make of the car on the rack, Jake had turned to run through the opened door of the workshop. Before he was halfway to the house, gunfire had erupted inside it, shattering the rural stillness. Behind him he could hear the deputy's footsteps following him across the hard-packed earth of the path that connected the two buildings.

When he reached the house, the front door was partially open. A glance at its broken lock told him that Billy had gotten his wish.

Jake put his shoulder against it, his weapon held in both hands. He turned to watch the deputy slide into place behind him.

When Blake nodded, Jake pushed the door wide and barreled through, leading with the Kimber. On some level, as he visually searched the cluttered front room, he was aware of the smell here, too. The same miasma of must and rot they'd encountered in the shop, compounded by the stench of unwashed humanity.

Trailed by the deputy, he moved forward, stepping over and around piles of dishes, food wrappers and scattered clothing. Despite the missing slats in the old-fashioned Venetian blinds, the moonlight made little headway against the grime-covered windowpanes.

Glancing over his shoulder, he motioned the other man toward the dining room and kitchen. Without questioning his right to direct the operation, the deputy stepped around him to move carefully into the other room.

Jake considered the dimness of the hall that stretched in front of him. He could discern at least three doors leading off it, but all of them were dark, as well.

Where the hell are you, Eden?

After the initial burst of gunfire, there had been nothing. No shouted commands. No sounds at all since they'd entered the house.

Anxiety tightening his throat, he stepped forward. The farther he moved down the hallway, the darker his surroundings became.

The first room—a bedroom judging by the width of the shape against the far wall—seemed to be the source of the sour odor of perspiration. He moved across it toward the sprawl of pale sheets.

"Major?"

The whispered question held a quality of panic he'd heard too many times to mistake. The deputy had encountered something in his search that he didn't know how to handle.

Taking a final glance around the room he was in, Jake turned and, still leading with the Kimber, headed back down the hall. The deputy stood at its end, silhouetted against the faint moonlight coming into the living room.

As Jake approached, he could see the guy was shaken. "What's wrong?"

"It's Billy. I think he's dead."

"Where?"

"Kitchen. There's blood all over the floor."

"And the chief?"

"I don't know. There's nobody else in there."

Jake pushed by him, unworried now about alerting the man they'd come to find. The possibilities ran through his head as he made his way across the dining room.

Maybe Eden had been wounded and was afraid now to

call out and reveal her location. She might be hiding from whoever had killed Billy. Or she might be under the control of that person, who he had to assume at this point was David Porter.

Jake reached the kitchen as he enumerated the last of those scenarios. Although he bent to verify, there was little doubt, given the size of the dark puddle under the body of the man lying on the cracked linoleum, that the deputy's assessment had been correct. Billy Gibbons was dead.

And there was no sign of what had happened to Eden.

Chapter Eighteen

When she came to, Eden was being dragged backward through palmetto and needlerush. She turned her head to vomit, but that didn't deter her attacker.

Hands locked under her breasts, he pulled her ruthlessly over the uneven ground, her heels bumping as if she were a rag doll carried by a careless child. Above her head, she could hear his breath sawing in and out as he struggled to draw her ever deeper into the vegetation.

She swallowed, trying to get enough saliva into her mouth to call out. The sound she managed was little more than a croak, but it evoked a response.

"Shut up," her captor hissed into her ear. "You shut the hell up, or I swear you'll be sorry you were born."

As if to emphasize the threat, one hand tightened painfully around her breast and twisted it. For a moment that unexpected agony overcame the chorus of pain throbbing at the back of her head.

She bit her bottom lip to control the urge to scream. Hot tears leaked from under her lids.

Dean had been right. She had botched this from the beginning. Billy was dead. And the man who'd shot him—

She realized that she had no idea what her captor intended to do with her. Or why he hadn't already killed her as he had Billy.

Porter didn't need a hostage. He had a far more valuable bargaining chip in the child. Unless...

Had they figured this out too late? Had he already disposed of the little girl? That would fit with what he had done in the other two cases Jake had found.

Jake.

Nothing had been said between them. No promises made. Other than the one she had felt so strongly in the few minutes he'd held her tonight. And now none of those possibilities would come to pass.

Not if she let Porter do whatever he wanted to her.

Even if she didn't understand his purpose in bringing her with him, she knew that eventually he would kill her. Just as he had killed Billy and other little girls.

And Raine? Dear God, had he already killed Raine?

As she enumerated the toll David Porter's bloodlust had taken, the thought that he might get away with it all fueled her sense of desperation.

She had no doubt Jake and Marty would come after them. They would have heard the blast that killed Billy, and they would come to find her. If she could slow Porter down, just long enough...

She turned her head again, pretending to wretch. With the shadows, she prayed that her captor wouldn't be able to tell she was faking.

"Please," she whispered. "Please, just... Just give me a minute. Please."

The response she expected was more pain. A blow to her aching head or some other sadistic attempt to shut her up. Instead, the hands that had been holding her upright released. She didn't have to fake her collapse onto the ground.

Behind her she could hear Porter fighting to control his ragged breathing. He was a strong man, but even for someone acclimated to the heat and humidity, dragging over a hundred pounds of essentially dead weight was physically exhausting.

Now, while he was at his most vulnerable, was the time to strike. She rolled to her side, trying to force her unresponsive limbs to obey. Ignoring the continuing agony in her head, she finally managed to get a knee under her.

"Stay down," Porter ordered, putting his booted foot on her back to push her to the ground. "You just stay still, you hear me."

She nodded, knowing that in her condition she posed no threat to him. The most she could hope for was to delay him long enough for Jake and whoever answered her radio call to catch up with them. And she had no idea how much of a head start they had.

"Where's Raine?" Her voice sounded as weak as her body felt.

"Shut up."

"Is she dead? Did you kill her, Dave?"

"I told you to shut the hell up." He took a menacing step toward her, his foot back, as if he intended to kick her in the ribs.

To her disgust, Eden cringed. However her intellect might urge her to respond, the most primitive part of her brain had a very clear memory of the kind of pain he was capable of inflicting. Like a burned child, she tried to avoid a repetition.

After a moment she gathered what remained of her courage to ask, "Where are you taking me?"

"Somewhere nobody'll ever find you, I can tell you that."

The words didn't seem like a threat. They felt more as if he were simply stating a truth. One he was willing to share with her because he believed there was nothing she could do to prevent him from carrying it out.

He bent to put his hand around her arm and pulled her up. Although she was glad of his help, she realized when she was on her feet how unsteady she was.

Concussion, she diagnosed. She'd seen enough football

players at the local high school react the same way after a hard hit to know what was wrong.

She also knew that many of those kids had returned to the game. Which was exactly what she had to do.

No matter how she felt, she had to fight. Her life—maybe Raine's as well—depended on it.

"Come on," Porter prodded. "You can walk."

She discovered that she could. And with each step she took she grew less disoriented. More confident in her ability to disrupt whatever he was planning to do. If she died in the attempt—

She blocked that thought, concentrating instead on the terrain they were passing through. Nothing about it looked familiar except the lush vegetation, which was exactly the same as that growing around the slough behind her house.

She didn't know how far from Porter's compound they had come, but eventually here, as almost anywhere in town, they would run into the water. And that would provide Porter with a far quicker means of transport than he'd been able to manage up until now.

Now. It had to be now.

She jerked free of the somewhat slackened hold he had on her left arm. As Porter began to turn toward her, eyes widened in surprise, she drove the heel of her right hand as hard as she could into his nose.

His head snapped back with the blow, his arms coming up automatically to protect his face. As they did, she moved in to slam her knee into his groin.

He bent forward in response, air rushing out of his mouth in a long exhalation. Even in his extremity, his hand reached for her, fingers like talons as they grasped the front of her shirt.

She tried to pull away, but his grip was too strong, as was the sturdy cotton blend of her uniform. Head still down, he held on as she beat at his face with both fists, trying desperately to break free.

He brought up the gun he held in his right hand, attempting to use the weapon like a club against the side of her face. She dodged backward to avoid the blow, dragging him with her. In attempting to regain his balance, his grasp loosened enough for the fabric of her shirt to slip between his fingers.

Eden turned and ran. The first bullet hit a tree in front of her, sending down a shower of bark. The resulting surge of adrenaline sent her scrambling over the massive trunk of a fallen pine, which received Porter's second shot.

As soon as her feet hit the ground on the other side, she made a turn to the right, putting the bulk of the tree's brown-needled branches between them. She plunged into the deeper shadows under the forest's canopy, always conscious of the noise she was making while listening for the sounds of pursuit.

Her boots splashed through shallow water, causing her to veer sharply to the left in an attempt to avoid whatever backwater she'd stumbled onto. In the darkness, she had lost all sense of direction. She had no idea if she was running toward the people who would be searching for her, or if she was simply running in a circle that would take her back to where she had begun. Back to Raine's kidnapper.

She slowed, trying to drag air into her aching lungs. And that was all she could hear, she realized. The sound of her own breathing.

Emboldened, she eased to a stop behind one of the towering pines and held her breath. The night creatures, aware of her presence, had fallen silent.

To her right, she heard a small splash as something slid into the water. Not Porter. And despite the dangers she knew were out here, there was nothing else she feared right now.

Again, she tried to figure out where she was. The moon, which had earlier tonight illuminated the landscape, was hidden by the trees above her head. She needed to find a clearing, somewhere she could get her bearings.

She began to move again, no longer running, having more confidence that her captor wasn't in the vicinity. Maybe he'd even given her up as lost.

For a few seconds that thought was comforting. Until she realized its implications for the little girl she had sought to save.

If she was right about Porter having a boat, then he would use it to disappear. And all chance of finding Raine, or at least finding out what had happened to her, would disappear with him.

She slowed, weighing the sanity of what she was thinking. Traumatic brain injury, Jake had called it. And Doc had echoed its probable side effects.

Despite the very real possibility that the blow to the head she'd received was clouding her judgment, she stopped and turned around, again trying to get her bearings. She looked up through the trees and saw the full moon floating above the clouds.

Exactly where she saw it when she looked up at Porter as she'd lain on the ground at his feet. She began to run toward it.

Back in the direction from which she'd come.

"HERE." BLAKE POINTED his flashlight downward. "He's still dragging her."

He was dragging something, Jake acknowledged, looking down at the trail of broken fronds they'd followed from Porter's house. He clung to the thought that, if Eden was dead, Porter wouldn't have bothered to carry her body with him.

He still believed that. He just couldn't figure out why the kidnapper would burden himself with her.

He pushed through the undergrowth, staying as close as

possible to the exact path the deputy was forging. Although here were no traps or mines out here, old habits died hard.

A few feet ahead of him, Blake froze. With his free hand he motioned Jake down. He obeyed instantly, hearing the sound that had alerted the other man that they were not alone.

From his vantage point, he watched as a darker shape moved ahead of them like a shadow through the dense vegetation. Without waiting for further communication from his companion, Jake began to circle noiselessly into a position behind whoever was out there.

He was close enough that he could hear the sounds of his prey's passage through the foliage. Not Eden, he assessed. The bulk and height was all wrong. And the only other person that they knew was out here was Porter.

He raised his weapon, sighting on the shadow that slipped from tree to tree. And then he waited for the representative of the law to do his thing.

"Put your hands up," the deputy barked finally.

The man they'd been watching spun instead, getting off a round in the direction of that disembodied voice. Jake's finger closed over the trigger, squeezing off a shot targeted at the muzzle flash.

Then he fired another, lowering his aim slightly. He didn't want to kill the bastard before he told them what he'd done with Eden.

The second bullet had the desired result, dropping Porter to his knees. Jake closed in rapidly behind him, pressing the muzzle of the Kimber against the back of his head.

"Drop it," he demanded.

When Porter tried to turn instead, Jake chopped downward with his weapon, catching him at the vulnerable juncture of neck and shoulder. His gun fell as the man's arm and hand went numb.

"Blake?" Jake called. "You hit?"

"I'm okay. You got him."

"Yeah," Jake affirmed softly, resisting the urge to tighter his finger over the trigger. Having read the files on wha Porter had done to the children he'd kidnapped, the temptation to kill him was almost biblical.

"Where is she?" he asked instead, increasing the pressure on the back of the man's head so that he was forced to bow it.

"I don't know what you're talking about."

"To be clear, right now I'm talking about Chief Reddick We'll get to the girl soon enough."

Porter's only response was a shake of his head. To his right Jake could hear the deputy moving toward them. He didn' take his eyes off the man kneeling at his feet.

"We know you dragged her out here with you. We followee the trail you left."

"Now why would I do something stupid as that?" Porte made no attempt to hide his sarcasm.

"Maybe because you *are* stupid," Blake said, as he stoppee beside them.

Jake looked up to assess the deputy's condition. He wa: holding one hand over the spreading bloodstain high on the opposite shoulder. Although Jake couldn't be certain whethe it was the result of blood loss or a trick of the moonlight, hi: face seemed to have lost all color.

"Sit down before you fall down," he suggested.

"I'm okay," Blake lied.

Faintly, in the distance, they heard the sound of sirens. Jak listened a moment to be sure that they were indeed headee for Porter's homestead.

"Last chance," he said, applying pressure again against the back of the kidnapper's neck with the muzzle of his weapon

"For what?"

"To tell me where they are?"

"They?" Despite the threat of the gun, Porter turned hi

head to look up at Jake. The moonlight on his upturned face revealed his amusement.

"Chief Reddick. And Raine Nolan."

As their eyes locked, Porter's mocking smile widened. Without another word, Jake redirected the muzzle of the Kimber so that it lay against the top of his shoulder.

He left it there long enough to see confusion replace the mockery in the dark eyes. Then he allowed his finger to tighten over the trigger.

The confusion was replaced by shock as the bullet tore through flesh and shattered bone. And then the man at his feet screamed.

"Words," Jake urged softly. "I need to hear words."

"I don't know where she is," Porter sobbed. "She got away. She ran off."

"In what direction."

"Back toward the house."

Jake moved the muzzle into position against the opposite shoulder.

"Hey," the deputy protested. "Hey, man, you can't do that."

"*You* can't do it," Jake said. "Everybody I ever answered to is dead."

"No matter what you think about him, he's our prisoner now. He's got rights." Despite spouting the correct words and phrases, Blake didn't sound convinced.

"He's killed at least twice. Innocent children. Defenseless little girls. Personally, I think he's forfeited any rights he might once have had."

The deputy's eyes were wide in the darkness. Jake knew exactly what he was wondering, but all he cared about right now was having time enough to finish what he'd started.

"So, how about Raine?" he prodded. "She 'run off,' too?"

Porter was still sobbing, the sound of his crying interspersed with curses. "Make the bastard stop," he pled with the deputy.

"You want me to stop, tell me where to find Raine Nolan."

"Do something," Porter begged.

"I suggest you tell him what he wants to know," Blake said. "They say he's crazy. I'm not certain they aren't right."

Jake waited while the man at his feet thought about it. He wasn't totally sure he wanted Porter to break so soon. There had been an unholy sense of satisfaction putting a bullet into his shoulder. The sirens had stopped, however, and he knew these woods would soon be full of people who might not share Blake's pragmatism.

"I can show you," Porter said. "Just...just don't shoot me again."

"She alive?" Jake held his breath as he waited for the response.

"The last time I saw her."

Jake didn't waste time asking when that was. He knew it had been at least forty-eight hours ago. And through how many of those had she been without food and water, alone in that terrifying darkness?

"Then the quicker you get us there," he said as he pulled Porter to his feet, "the better it's going to be for everybody. Especially for you."

Chapter Nineteen

The reinforcements she'd called for had found Eden before she'd caught up with Porter. Given her condition at that point, she knew she should be grateful it had worked out that way.

One of the deputies had accompanied her back to Porter's place, where Dean had set up a command center. Her deputy chief had taken one look at her and demanded that the paramedics check her out.

She was still sitting on the tailgate of their van when Dean came to find her. She could tell by his expression that things had taken a step in the right direction.

"They've got him," he said. "Blake just radioed in. He's taking them to where he's been keeping Raine."

"Is she...?" she hesitated, unwilling to put the fear she knew they all shared into words.

"They don't know. Porter says she was all right the last time he saw her."

"I need to be there." She tried to stand, but swayed as soon as she made it to her feet.

"No, you don't." Dean took her elbow to steady her.

It was hard to argue with his assessment. Despite the blanket the paramedic had wrapped around her shoulders, she hadn't been able to stop shaking. Maybe the aftereffects of her head injury. Adrenaline overload. Exhaustion. A combination of all of them.

It was clear from the look in Dean's eyes what his diagnosis would be. Right now, she didn't care what he or anyone else thought.

She needed to be there when they found Raine. No matter the outcome.

"Get a location," she ordered.

"Eden—"

"Are the two of them okay? Marty. And Major Underwood?"

"Blake's got a flesh wound. Underwood seems to have taken command."

That would be a natural role for Jake. And she couldn't think of anyone she'd rather have in charge of this operation.

"Marty's got to have some idea where they are. He knows this area as well as anyone."

"He thinks Porter's following Birdwell Creek."

The creek, like all of those in this region, would eventually lead to the estuary. "Then we can get there faster by boat."

"If we had one," Dean said.

"Have somebody get one out here. We don't have any way to know what shape that child may be in. And Marty's been wounded. It just makes sense, Dean."

She couldn't be sure his hesitation in acting on her suggestion was because he thought it a bad idea, or, as she suspected, that because of her condition, he believed he was better equipped to make those kinds of decisions.

Although she didn't see the value of debating the point in the middle of an operation, she also believed she had to speak to the needs of a terrified little girl. Something the men in her department might not assign as high a priority.

"You sit back down and let these guys take care of you, and I'll get a boat out here," Dean said finally, perhaps reading the determination in her eyes.

Having won the point, she nodded, but even that slight movement set off the pounding in her skull. She eased back down onto the liftgate, watching Dean walk toward the others, his radio in his hand.

"He's been very concerned about you."

She glanced up at the paramedic who had given her the blanket. "He's known me most of my life. At times, he still thinks I need taking care of."

"At *times,* we all do. This might be one of them."

She couldn't argue with that. And she was grateful for Dean's calm leadership in this situation. Even if she had a feeling most of the men he'd brought out here with him felt the same way.

"THAT'S IT."

Dave Porter didn't look at Jake as he indicated the small building constructed of cement blocks. He had avoided making eye contact since Jake had dragged him to his feet and pushed him in the direction he'd been headed when they'd captured him.

"Key," Jake demanded.

The door was closed with a padlock pushed through the rusted hasp. Although there were two windows on the front of the structure, they had long ago been boarded over.

"In my pocket." Porter made no move to retrieve it, continuing to hold his left hand under the elbow of the arm Jake had used for target practice.

"I'm not getting it out for you." To emphasize his point, Jake lifted his weapon.

The mechanic grimaced as he released the injured arm and flattened his left hand to dig into the pocket of his jeans. He held out the key, but Jake found it almost impossible to cross the short distance that separated them to take it.

He'd seen death in almost every guise, none of them pleasant, but the thought of what he might find inside when he unlocked that door turned his stomach. Only the possibility that Raine might be still alive gave him the courage to reach out and snatch the key from the oil-stained fingers.

Ignoring everything but the task at hand, an art he'd learned early in his career, he lifted the lock and inserted the key. Despite its obvious age, the mechanism moved smoothly, snapping open in his hand. He slipped the padlock out of the loop and pulled the hasp away.

No sound came from inside. Certainly not the heartbroken crying he'd heard in his flashback.

"Major?" Blake's voice sounded as shaken as he felt.

"Yeah." Steeling himself for what he might find, Jake opened the door.

The stench from inside was strong, but not the one he'd dreaded. Not the unforgettable smell of a decomposing body, a process that wouldn't take long in this heat.

"Flashlight?"

Without turning away from the black opening before him, Jake held out his hand to the deputy. He heard Blake move behind him, and then felt the solid weight of the light from the deputy's utility belt hit his palm. He fumbled a moment with the switch, and then taking a step forward, directed the beam into the low interior.

It was exactly as it had been in his flashback. Dank and dark and malodorous. And in the farthermost corner, against the block wall, was a huddled shape.

The child appeared no larger than the doll he'd removed from Eden's bed. Her head rested on her chest, matted blond hair falling forward onto the front of her dirty nightgown.

Jake could detect no movement. Not even the rise and fall of the small arms that were crossed over her stomach.

"Major?"

Again, Blake's question drove him to take the next step. He walked across the dirt floor and squatted in front of the girl. "Raine?"

There was no response.

Jake didn't want to frighten her if she was simply asleep, but he knew he didn't have a choice about what he had to do next. He slipped two fingers under her hair and placed them on the side of her neck.

Before he could locate the pulse he sought, she cringed, pressing her spine against the wall behind her. As her head came up, she blinked against the light he held and then raised one hand to shield her eyes.

"It's okay," Jake said softly. "We've come to take you home. You want to go home to your mommy?"

The blue eyes clung to his face as her arm slowly lowered. He couldn't tell if the dark spot on her cheek was dirt or a bruise. The thought that it might be the latter made him wish once more that Porter hadn't caved so quickly.

"You want to go home?" he asked again.

"I thought you were coming to get me before."

The words were so soft Jake figured he must have mistaken them. "You thought I was coming?"

She nodded. With that movement he could see the paler tracks of tears through the dirt on her face.

"I was," he said, laying the flashlight on the ground beside his boot. "I was coming to find you all along. And now I'm here."

She nodded again, and then the small arms reached up to him. Whatever additional reassurances he'd planned to offer about taking her to her mother were blocked by the thickness of the knot in his throat.

"Is she in there?" Blake called. "Is she—"

"She's here. She's okay." As Jake scooped her up, Raine's arms fastened around his neck. She buried her face against his shoulder. Her filthy hair still smelled faintly of strawberries.

He ducked his head as they emerged from the low doorway. Blake's face reflected the same joy and relief Jake had felt, but his weapon was still trained on the man who'd brought them here.

"I can't believe it," the deputy breathed. "Damn, I can't believe she's alive."

"Let's get her out of here."

"They're on their way with a boat. It'll be quicker."

"That's good." The sooner they got her away from this place, the sooner someone could begin work to erase the memories of what had happened to her. And seeing Porter, he realized, wouldn't be helpful in that regard.

He put his hand on the back of Raine's head, hoping that would encourage her to keep her face against his shoulder. He moved past the kidnapper, resisting the urge to shoot the bastard again. This time, just for the sheer pleasure of it.

"You did good work tonight," Blake said. "Whatever it took... It was worth it."

Jake nodded as he kept walking, but the lump was back in his throat.

EDEN HAD REFUSED the entreaties of the paramedics to lie down on the cot in back of their van. Only when they'd promised to let her know as soon as the rescue party returned, had she agreed to rest in the reclining passenger seat up front.

After an eternity, the EMT who'd been treating her stuck his head in the open window. "They're back. You feel up to getting out?"

She nodded, aware for the first time that whatever he'd given her for the pain must have some narcotic properties, as well. As she began to climb down from the high seat, he, too, took her arm to steady her.

"Raine?"

"They got her. My partner's going to check her out more thoroughly as soon as they get here." They walked toward the lights the department had set up in the clearing around Porter's house, his hand still supporting her. "But I understand from the deputies that your guy thinks she's going to be okay."

Your guy. It took a couple of seconds before she realized he was referring to Marty Blake rather than Jake. And another few before the import of what he'd just said caused her eyes to sting with tears.

"You all right?"

"Just emotional," she confessed.

"I think everybody is."

"It's the best outcome we could have hoped for." One she would not have dreamed possible twenty-four hours ago.

For some reason, she lifted her gaze across the clearing. Jake was coming toward them, Raine Nolan held securely in the crook of his elbow. The child had one arm around his shoulders. The other rested across his broad chest.

The tears Eden had blinked away would no longer be denied. There was something incredible about the absolute trust this little girl, who had been through such a terrible ordeal, was able to give to a complete stranger.

A stranger who had been relentless from the first in his determination to find her and bring her home. No matter the cost.

Margo Nolan stepped out of the crowd to move toward Jake, who was trailed by the deputies who had brought them here. Halfway there, she broke into a run.

As soon as Raine saw her, she reached out, almost diving into Margo's arms. Eden knew she wasn't the only one in the crowd whose vision blurred again as they watched that reunion.

When Ray joined them, he took a moment to say something to the man who had carried his daughter. Jake shook his head, squeezing Nolan's shoulder before he used that same hand to turn him toward his wife and child.

Then he walked past them, his eyes searching the crowd. When they found her, it was as if Eden could literally feel the intensity of his gaze. Unlike Margo, he didn't increase his speed as he came toward her, his limp more pronounced than it had ever been before.

Eden began to move across the clearing, uncaring who might witness their meeting. As if by mutual agreement, they stopped with a scant yard between them. Jake's eyes continued to search her face, before he reached out to gently caress her temple with his thumb.

With the ongoing agony at the back of her skull, Eden had forgotten Porter had struck her there. Apparently, even in this light, Jake could see the bruise his blow had caused.

She caught his hand, aware again of the tensile strength of his fingers. "It's okay."

"Are *you?*"

"I am now."

She didn't elaborate on whether that was a reference to Raine's recovery, to Porter's capture or to the fact that they were again together, both having survived a situation in which others had not. She simply stepped into his arms, exactly as she had earlier tonight.

They closed around her as they had then. Her cheek against his chest, she could feel the steady rhythm of his heartbeat.

After a moment she raised her head to look up into his eyes. At what she saw in them, her lips parted, anticipating the feel of his mouth over hers.

"Chief?"

Dean. Duty.

Reluctantly, she began to straighten away from Jake's embrace. Without a word, he released her, stepping back to put more distance between them.

"What is it?" Her voice sounded strained to her own ears.

"WXZO is here. They want to do an interview with the Nolans, and then they want to talk to you. To get a rundown on the rescue."

She looked back at Jake, whose face reflected nothing of what she was feeling. "It's you they'll want to talk to."

He shook his head. "I'm not law enforcement."

"But you *are* Raine's rescuer."

"No more than you. Or Blake."

"I don't even know how you found Porter. Or convinced him to take you to her. Law enforcement or not, you're the one who can give them those kinds of details."

He held her eyes for a moment. "Somebody else needs to handle the press. I'm not going to speak for the department." His lips tightened before he added, "And maybe it's better you don't have those details."

"What does that mean?" Dean asked.

Jake ignored the question. "You can tell them that after Porter was taken into custody, he revealed the girl's location to Deputy Blake."

"You think *Marty* ought to talk to them?" There was some undercurrent in his voice she couldn't read.

"*You're* the chief of police." He nodded at Dean and then walked on past them.

Eden waited until Jake was out of earshot before she asked, "You think I offended him? I know he's not the kind to seek the limelight, but…"

"I don't think he was offended."

"Something's going on. I'm just not sure what."

"I think maybe you ought to do what the man told you to. *Exactly* what he told you. They're waiting." Dean inclined his head.

Eden looked in the direction he'd indicated to see the woman who anchored the nightly news interviewing Margo, who was holding Raine as if she would never let go. Ray was nowhere in sight.

There were only a few people in this world that Eden respected enough to obey without question. And two of them had just told her the same thing.

With that in mind, she started toward the portable klieg lights the local station had set up for their reporter. She couldn't do anything about the torn uniform or the bruises on her face, but as she walked, Eden finger-combed her hair away from her face, trying to restore some sense of order, even if only in her own mind.

Margo smiled at her. Seeing the mother's expression, the anchor seemed to realize that her audience would probably enjoy watching the first meeting between the two of them and beckoned Eden into the frame.

"Chief Reddick, can you tell us what led you to suspect David Porter? How did your department zero in on him as the kidnapper?"

"We had some preliminary evidence that Porter might be implicated in other child abductions that had occurred in nearby states. When we came out to question him about those and about a pending assault charge, he opened fire, killing one of my deputies."

"I understand that he also took you hostage for a period."

"It's possible he thought he could use me as some kind of bargaining chip. Or as a shield. We aren't sure of his motivations at this time."

"You escaped, and some of your deputies were later able to capture the kidnapper. Is that right?"

"That's correct. And once Porter was in custody, he revealed Raine's location to a deputy." As she repeated Jake's words, she again tried to put her finger on what bothered her about them.

"I know you and your men have worked day and night on this case. And I'm sure no one, other than Raine's family of course, could be happier with its outcome. Mrs. Nolan, is there anything you'd like to say to Chief Reddick and her department?"

Margo leaned her cheek against her daughter's head. "I want to say thank-you to everyone who helped search for Raine. The people of Waverly, the police department, the agents from the Bureau. And especially to Major Underwood," she added. "After all, he's the one who brought Raine home and put her back in my arms."

The reporter turned toward Eden, her well-shaped brows lifted in question. "Major Underwood?"

"One of the many people in Waverly who devoted their time to finding Raine." Eden reached out and touched the child's grubby fingers. "And we're all very glad she's home safe and sound, and with her family tonight."

She turned and moved away from the lights and the camera. Behind her she could hear the reporter pose a question to Raine and the child's treble voice as she answered it.

Whatever the little girl had suffered, given the resiliency of childhood and the love of her family, she would eventually recover. Margo's initial surety about her daughter's response to being kidnapped had apparently been correct.

Even that comforting thought didn't erase the troubling feeling that Jake, and even Dean, were keeping something from her. And right now, she didn't see either of them among the crowd.

As her eyes surveyed the area, she saw that Marty Blake was being treated by the same paramedic who'd tended her earlier. She walked over to them, putting that worrisome question aside for now. The deputy looked up to smile at her.

"Porter told us you'd gotten away. I wasn't sure he was telling the truth until I saw you out there." He nodded toward the reporter and Margo, who had finally been joined by her husband.

"Considering what he did to your chief," the paramedic said, "she's lucky to be able to do that."

"What did he do?"

Blake's concern had been immediate as well as genuine. Maybe, she comforted herself, not all of her men would rather have Dean at the helm.

"I've been accused on more than one occasion of having a hard head. I guess those folks were right. How about you?" She looked to the EMT, rather than the deputy, to supply that information.

"He seems about as lucky as you."

"Good." She touched Blake's arm. "You did fine work tonight."

He ducked his head, embarrassed by the compliment. "Everybody did. I'm just sorry about Billy."

She nodded, again thinking that she should have been the one to take the lead in the search of Porter's house. "At least Raine's safe. How'd you all convince him to give up her location? I figured he'd use that as a bargaining chip to avoid the chair. You make him any promises about that? Not that I'd blame you if you did."

Blake glanced up at the paramedic, who pretended not to be listening. "No promises," the deputy said. "You don't need to worry about that."

He hadn't really emphasized the last word. And maybe she was reading too much into Jake's behavior. The reporter hadn't questioned the story. Maybe no one would.

Despite that, she was certain something was going on. Something Marty and Jake knew, and Dean had figured out.

Something she needed to find out before she publicly answered any more questions about Raine Nolan's rescue.

Chapter Twenty

Jake had watched from the patrol car as Eden systematically completed all the tasks she needed to do before she could go home. The interview with the locals. Talking to her wounded deputy. Conferring with Dean about where they went from here. And because he had respect for her intelligence, he knew that the whole time she'd been doing those things, she'd been thinking about what he hadn't told her.

As she approached the cruiser where he was waiting, he tried, as he had for the last hour, to prepare himself for her reaction. He had even considered telling her nothing in response to the questions he expected her to ask.

All he wanted to do—had wanted to do since she had melted against him outside her house tonight—was to hold her. Actually, that was about as far removed from what he wanted to do as the story he'd given her for the press was from the truth.

When Eden opened the car door, the dome light overhead came on. With its illumination, her eyes considered his face, seeming to ask the questions she hadn't yet put into words.

He refused to look away. He had done what the situation called for. He might regret that he'd had to do it, but he didn't regret its outcome. For most of his professional life, that had been all that mattered to him.

He wasn't sure that was true anymore. Not if it destroyed what had been developing between him and Eden.

"Get in," he said.

"The EMT told me not to get behind the wheel for the next twenty-four hours."

"We can trade places later. Or somebody else can drive you home," he added, watching for her reaction.

After a moment she dropped her eyes and crawled in beside him. When she closed the door, the resulting darkness provided both privacy and a strange sense of intimacy.

She turned to look at him, her disordered hair framing the pale oval of her face. Her eyes widened as he leaned across the console. Despite her surprise, her lips parted, just as they had before, inviting his kiss.

His conscience argued that he owed her an explanation before he took this any further. He ignored all the good reasons for doing that.

This might be the last opportunity he'd have to tell her something that, to him at least, was far more important than what he'd done to Porter. He put his hand at the back of her neck, gently drawing her to him.

Their lips met, hers soft and trembling. Her tongue touched his, her response to his kiss more than he'd dared to hope it might be.

The restraint he'd been determined to show evaporated at his first taste of her mouth. Sweet, hot and clearly hungry for this. Just as he was.

His hand moved down her spine, urging a closer contact between them. Her arms came around his neck as she deepened the kiss. Lost in the feel of her body against his, he didn't want to let her go, afraid this would never happen again.

She was the one who ended it, finally leaning back to look up into his eyes again. "That's been a long time coming."

"I wasn't sure how welcome it would be."

Her brows lifted. "Because...?"

He laughed, thinking of all the very good reasons not to let her know how he felt. "I carry a lot of baggage."

"Everybody does."

She meant her sister's kidnapping, he supposed. Her mother's suicide, perhaps. All of which had impacted her life. And had made her who she was. On the other hand...

"Maybe. But..." He hesitated.

"What is it?"

"You've heard the things people here have said about me."

"So?"

"Most of them are true."

"*Most* of what I've heard had to do with your military record. You served our country honorably." She took a breath, deep enough to be visible. "And you paid a price."

"Some people might dispute that."

She shook her head. "Dispute what?"

"Honorably can be subjective."

"Are you saying that you did things you regret?"

He thought about it before he answered. When he had, he told her the absolute truth. "No."

"Then...?"

"I did things others might regard as outside the boundaries of conventional warfare," he said carefully.

There was a long heartbeat before she asked, "What does that mean? Exactly."

"The unit I belonged to frequently operated outside the lines. We were assigned missions that nobody was ever going to write up in glowing terms for the newspapers. Things that had to be done, but that nobody wanted to take responsibility for doing."

"You did them."

"For most of my career."

"Against orders?"

"Our orders were fluid. We did what the situation called for. In our best judgment."

The silence this time went on longer than he wanted, despite how much he dreaded her next question. When it came, it was nothing he expected.

"Is that what you did tonight? What the situation called for?"

"I brought Raine home. In *my* best judgment, that outweighed every other consideration."

"You thought I'd second-guess that?"

"I don't want what I did to discredit you or the department."

"And Blake went along with what you did?"

"He protested that I was violating the prisoner's rights."

Her lips lifted slightly at the corners, but she quickly controlled the movement. "Then I think the department's covered. Jake, I don't care what you did to get Porter to talk. Whatever it was, it wasn't nearly what the bastard deserved."

"His lawyer will care."

"Then we'll deal with that. When and if it happens. In all honesty, I don't think anything will come of this. Blake didn't even mention it to me. And believe me, if it ever comes to trial, no jury here is going to convict you, no matter what you had to do to find Raine. Most of those people out there—" she turned to look through the windshield "—would applaud you. Personally, I think we're all lucky you were the one in position to convince him."

He laughed, part relief and part genuine amusement at her assessment. Then he touched the bruise on her temple again. "It wasn't enough."

"Actually, I think this is the least of it." She put her fingers over his. "Invading my home. Taunting me…"

The scenario she was describing was one he'd had a problem with all along. He still couldn't see Porter taking chances like that.

"You sure he did those things?"

Her eyes widened again, this time in confusion. "Who else could it have been?"

"You think Porter had something to do with your sister's kidnapping? How old would he have been at that time?"

"I don't know. I don't know how old he is now, but..." She shook her head again. "Nothing else makes sense."

"It didn't from the beginning. I can buy Porter's attack on me. Whether anybody else believed what I was saying about where Raine was being held, he *knew* that what I saw was too close to reality to ignore. He had to shut me up. I think he was hoping for more help from the crowd than he got that day, but the other...? Either Porter was involved with your sister's disappearance, or he did a hell of a job researching something you say nobody here knew anything about."

"But...if it wasn't Porter, then who? And more important, why?"

"I can't answer that. With Porter in custody, we may never know."

"You don't believe there will be any more incidents."

That hadn't been phrased as a question, but he treated it as one. "I think, for one thing, it would be too dangerous to continue with the kidnapper behind bars. For another, what would be the purpose?"

"I'm not sure I understood the purpose before."

"I think you were right. Whoever this was intended to interfere in the investigation."

"Thanks to you, he didn't succeed."

"But that's what he was hoping for."

"To protect Porter? You think somebody else was in on this with him?"

"I don't know. Is there someone in town who's particularly close to him?"

Her eyes changed. She opened her mouth and then closed it. "I can't believe he'd be involved in something like that."

"Maybe he didn't understand the significance of what he was doing. Maybe he thought of it as a prank. Or maybe he was so under Porter's thumb, he never questioned whatever he told him to do."

When Eden didn't respond, he added the caveat he himself had just realized. "That doesn't explain, however, how Porter knew about your sister."

"You're the one who said the information was out there. That everything's on the web."

"It is. But you have to know how and where to look for it."

Her eyes met his. "Not if you have access to the official databases that contain all the details about cold cases."

THE POLICE STATION had been virtually deserted when they left. Now it was filled with people, despite the fact that at least half the small force was still working the two crime scenes.

Without a word, Eden motioned for the kid at the front desk to follow them back to her office. After a moment's hesitation, he complied.

"Close the door," she ordered as he entered.

He glanced at Jake before he obeyed. With the noise from the front room muted, Eden let the tension build a moment.

The kid clearly knew that he was here because of his association with Porter. What else he knew was still in question.

"If I'd had any idea what kind of guy—" he began.

"You been in my house lately, Carl?"

Something that looked like genuine confusion appeared in the boy's eyes. "Ma'am?"

"Have you been in my house? You know, broken into it?"

He glanced at Jake again, as if to ask whether or not this was some kind of joke. When Jake kept his face expressionless, Carl looked back at Eden.

"I don't think I've ever been in your house, Chief. And I damn sure haven't *broken* in. There or anywhere else."

The deputy's face had flushed with what Jake would bet was genuine indignation. It was obvious Carl was struggling for control.

"Maybe trying to help your friend out a little? Generate a minor distraction in the middle of an investigation?"

"I don't have any idea what you're talking about, Chief. Dave was good to me. I consider—considered," he amended, "him a friend. But I never tried to help him with what he did to that little girl. I wouldn't do that. I wouldn't have anything to do with hurting a child."

"How about just playing a few tricks on your boss? Everybody's wanted to do that at times."

"No, ma'am. I don't have any reason to do something like that. I like you. I like working here. Why would I do something that stupid?"

"I don't know. All I know is that somebody did. And that you've acknowledged you were close to Porter."

"I'm not the only person in this town who thought of Dave as a friend."

"No, but you're one of the few with access to this office."

The kid's brow furrowed. "You think I gave him information about the investigation?" He shook his head. "You've known me all of my life, Chief. You know my mama and daddy. You really think I'd do something to help a man who—" he paused, seeming to search for terminology "—who does that to little girls?"

Several seconds ticked by as the boy's question went unanswered. "I want you to go on home," Eden said finally. "Go home and stay there. Don't talk to anybody. That's an order, Carl. You understand me?"

"Yes, ma'am." The kid's face was tight with indignation, but he worked manfully for control. "Is that all?"

"For now." The boy turned on his heel and had made it to the door before Eden spoke again. "If I'm wrong, Carl, then I'm sorry. There are just..." This time she was the one who searched for words. "A lot of things have been happening around here that I have no explanation for."

Carl nodded, his eyes holding hers. "I understand that, but

you ought to know me well enough to know that whatever the explanation is, I'm not it."

With that he was gone, closing the door carefully behind him so that his outrage wouldn't be apparent, other than in his heartfelt self-defense.

Eden turned to Jake. "What do you think?"

"I don't think he had a clue what you were talking about."

She took a breath. "We need to check the computer out front to make sure. I'm not good enough to do much beyond pulling up the search history, but the boys from Jackson should be able to verify if he was telling the truth. And honestly, for his mama's and daddy's sake, if for no other reason, I hope to God he was."

Jake nodded, reading exhaustion in her face. This was something that could wait. Whoever had been behind the scare tactics concerning her sister's kidnapping would have no reason now to continue them.

And if they were foolish enough to try, they were going to have him to contend with. Because there was no way he was going to leave her alone again.

Chapter Twenty-One

Almost too exhausted to think, and vastly relieved that for the first time in almost a week she didn't have to, Eden hadn't been aware of where they were going until Jake turned onto her street. She didn't want to go home, she realized. Not given the things that had happened there and the fact that the prankster apparently still had access to the house.

"Not here."

Jake turned to look at her. Even in the darkness she could read the question in his eyes.

"I can't sleep there."

She leaned back against the seat and closed her eyes. She didn't care where they spent the night. As long as they were together.

She sat up when the cruiser slowed again to find him turning into the long drive that led to his grandmother's house. He pulled the patrol car around to the back and then killed the engine.

After a moment the headlights went out, leaving them once more alone in a sheltering darkness. Gradually, in the stillness, the night creatures resumed their nighttime serenade.

"Your grandmother would be scandalized," she said.

"You can sleep in her room."

Jake got out, leaving her to think about what he'd said as

he walked around the front of the car. He opened her door, holding out his hand.

As she took it, she asked. "And what if I don't want to sleep in Miz Etta's room?"

The only answer was the slight tremor in the long brown fingers that closed around hers. But he didn't release her hand until they'd reached the front door.

When he'd unlocked it, Jake's palm settled against the small of her back to usher her inside. With the intimacy of that gesture, something happened deep within her body. A heated anticipation that made her heart rate accelerate and her breathing quicken.

Jake seemed not to notice. Or maybe, she conceded, he was accustomed to having that effect on women. After all, he was bound to be more experienced at this than she was.

When he'd closed the door and turned the dead bolt, he led the way through the house. A light burned somewhere in the back, but the front rooms were dark.

As her eyes adjusted, Eden contrasted the almost pristine condition of the place where he lived with the one they'd broken into tonight. And then, unwilling to allow any of those images into her brain, she banished that comparison.

What had happened at Porter's was something she would think about tomorrow. Tonight...

"You think Miz Etta's got a nightgown I could borrow?"

Jake's eyes were silver as he turned to look at her, his face as expressionless as it had been while she'd questioned Carl. "All her things are still in her room. I'm sure you can find something. Second door on the right." He tilted his head down the hall.

The light she'd noticed before was coming from the room on the left. Jake's bedroom? If so, it seemed he really did intend for them to occupy separate beds, despite her earlier attempt to suggest something else.

A suggestion he hadn't responded to, she reminded herself. "Thanks."

Humiliated, she began to move past him. His hand fastened around her upper arm, stopping her progress.

"We talked about baggage. Just not all of it."

"Something else in your sordid past I need to know about?" She smiled at him, just in case he might not realize she was teasing.

"Something in my present." He took her hand, placing it against the side of his head, just above the temple.

When she felt the depression in the bone, her first impulse was to pull her fingers away. Thankfully, she was able to control that reaction.

"The effects of this aren't ever going away, Eden. Not entirely."

"The flashbacks?"

"Those. The impulsivity, whatever the hell that means. Anger issues." He took a breath, deep enough to be visible. "The physical stuff."

She wasn't sure what he wanted her to say. To be honest, she wasn't sure how she felt about some of the things he'd mentioned.

The only thing she *was* sure of was how she felt about him. "It doesn't matter."

"It may."

"At some point in the future? I guess it might. I would think you, of all people, know that we can't predict what *might* happen. I could never have predicted my sister's kidnapping. Or my mother's reaction to it. Even my father's.

"The Nolans could never have dreamed their lives would be turned upside down in a single night. Or that a man who had visions of their daughter would rescue her. Life doesn't come with guarantees, Jake, so if a guarantee is what you're looking for from me—"

He put both hands on her shoulders, pulling her upward

so he could close her mouth with his. This kiss was nothing
like the one in the car. Now his lips possessed hers almost
ruthlessly. And when he was done, leaving her limp with need
and desire, he raised his head to look down into her eyes.

"You through?"

"With what?"

"Talking."

She nodded, reading the promise in his face.

"Good." He bent to slip his arm under her knees, picking
her up as if she weighed no more than the child he'd carried
across the clearing.

Remembering that scene, she, too, put her arms around
his neck and her head against his shoulder, trusting herself
to him completely.

EDEN CAME AWAKE gradually, a luxury she hadn't enjoyed in a
long time. Late-morning sunlight filtered into the room, but
the angle of it was wrong. Unfamiliar.

With that realization the memories of last night invaded
her consciousness. The horror at Porter's compound. Raine's
homecoming. Jake.

Jake.

She turned her head, made aware by that movement of the
muscled arm it rested against, and found herself face-to-face
with the man who'd made love to her last night with a tender-
ness she had never expected. And would always cherish.

His eyes held hers before they deliberately refocused on
her mouth. Remembering, as she knew he was, she smiled
at him.

"I should have shaved." His thumb moved back and forth
across her beard-burned chin.

"It's okay."

"Such soft skin." His thumb traced slowly down her throat.
At the bottom of his hand's descent, the tips of his extended
fingers brushed her breast, as if by accident.

Her nipple hardened in response. Physical memory? If so, it was even stronger than those embedded in her brain.

In how many ways had he touched her throughout the night? Teasing. Tantalizing. Teaching.

His fingers continued their seemingly aimless exploration, but she knew better. There was no doubt in her mind about what was about to happen.

Her mouth opened, breath sighing out in anticipation of what he would make her feel. He slipped his arm from under her head, turning to prop himself on his elbow in order to look down on her.

With his left hand he cupped her breast, lowering his head to run his tongue lazily around the areola. Again her nipple tightened, begging for his attention.

Jake complied, rimming the sensitive nub with moisture before his teeth closed gently over it. With that pressure, a surge of heat exploded deep within Eden's body.

Jake responded to her gasp by deserting her breast to trail featherlight kisses down her stomach. The small indentation of her belly button slowed his progress, seeming to demand a prolonged concentration.

And all the while, she knew his true intent. Anticipated it. Wanted it now with a desperation she had not known she could experience until he had made love to her.

Finally—finally—his lips slipped lower still. Her fingers locked into the coarseness of his hair as his tongue again began the assault she had resisted last night and now welcomed.

Its movements were delicate at first. And then, as with his kiss, it became demanding.

Sensation upon sensation shivered along nerve endings supplied by a generous nature for such an onslaught. The longer he touched her, the more urgently they reverberated. Controlling. Engulfing her, so that every particle of her being centered on one objective.

Her breathing grew ragged. Her fingers found the corded muscle of his shoulder, echoing the pressure building inside her straining body.

And when, after an eternity, it released, the wave of feeling was so intense it threatened to overwhelm her. To separate her consciousness from this. From him.

Jake didn't allow that to happen. As soon as he felt the tremor that signaled the culmination of what he had given her, he moved above her, his mouth closing over her parted lips.

The hard wall of his chest flattened her breasts. Her hands found his hips as she lifted her body to his.

Skin against dampened skin. His, hair-roughened. Unabashedly male.

And suddenly, despite what had just occurred, she wanted more. She wanted it all.

His heat and hardness inside her. Ravaging her body as his mouth continued to ravage hers.

Everything she had learned that he could give her, and more important now, everything that she had learned to give him.

Her legs opened to welcome him. And when he pushed into the heat and wetness he had created, her body responded, relaxing to accept him fully. Trying to become one with his.

As he slowly began to move above her, incredibly, she felt that infinite pleasure begin to build again. Her hips strained upward, seeking to match his movements with their own.

Joined with this one man in a union older than time, she was aware of nothing but Jake. Mindless with love and desire, she sought to bring him to completion.

And when the release he sought finally came, his frame was racked by its force. She clung to him, nails biting into the powerful muscles that continued to drive above her.

To fulfillment and beyond. More this time than she thought

she could bear. Her body echoed the explosion in his as the air thinned and darkened around them.

When it was over, they lay exhausted by what had just happened. Their panting bodies still joined. Still one.

Like waves retreating from shore, the internal sensations finally trembled into stillness. Eventually, their ragged breathing eased, too, and then slowed.

After a long time, Jake lifted his torso from hers, allowing the artificially cooled air to touch the dampness of her skin. She shivered, more an aftershock of what they'd shared than an expression of discomfort.

"Cold?" With one hand he reached back to pull the tangled sheet over them.

"Lonely."

The silver eyes came back to her face, questioning.

"Lonely for you," she clarified.

"I couldn't be closer."

"Not now. I think I've been lonely for you all my life."

As she said the words, she recognized their truth. She had been alone almost her entire life.

In the space of a year, she had lost her sister, her mother and her childhood. And although she had never doubted her father's love, she had gradually come to understand that his support and encouragement had been as much about insuring someone would continue his quest as helping her reach her own potential.

When Jake didn't respond to what she'd said, she knew she had stepped over the line they'd established last night.

"No pressure." She smiled at him as her fingers brushed along the trace of silver in the dark hair at his temple.

"It's not that. I just..." He shook his head. "Of all the lingering annoyances of the last year, it was the flashbacks I hated most."

Her face must have reflected her surprise, because he added, "They should have seemed minor, I guess, compared to the rest. But I've always valued control. Of myself. Of whatever situation I found myself in. After I was injured, I wasn't in control anymore. Not of my body. Not even of my memories."

She said nothing, knowing how hard this confession would be for the man he was.

He took another breath before he went on. "But the flashbacks... Seeing Raine in them... I don't have an explanation for how that was possible. I doubt I ever will. The ultimate loss of control, and yet...here we are."

"This wouldn't have happened except for those," she finished for him.

"For the first time, it all seems worth it."

Her eyes burned, but she denied the tears. He wasn't a man who would welcome sympathy. Not for anything he'd gone through.

"Full circle," she said softly.

His brow furrowed slightly as he shook his head again.

"My father's obsession. He didn't find Christie, but the files left from his search led to your recovery of Raine. I wasn't the investigator he wanted—someone like him, determined not to give up—but I respected him enough to keep the information he'd accumulated. And in the end..."

"A little girl came home because of it."

She didn't blink away the moisture that filled her eyes this time, because it was for her father and not for Jake. "A fitting legacy of a father's love."

"Who knows?" Jake used his thumb to wipe away an escaping tear. "Maybe they *all* had something to do with this. Guiding us. Watching over Raine."

"Do you believe that?" She would like to. It would help make what her family had endured mean something at last.

"I told you. I don't have an explanation. But to me...that's as good as any."

It was, she discovered. Something she would always hold on to as a connection to those she had loved and lost.

And a reminder, if she ever needed one, of how much they, too, had loved her. Another little girl who was also—finally—coming home.

Epilogue

"I've been meaning to call you. And then I run into you right here in the grocery store."

Eden looked up from the steaks she'd been trying to choose between to find Laurie Greene standing at her elbow. Acknowledging that this was probably the confrontation she'd been expecting for the past six weeks, she laid the packages she'd been considering back on the stack in the cooler.

"Hey, Laurie." Deliberately, Eden imbued her voice with a friendliness she didn't feel. "What can I do for you?"

Although she and Jake had tried to be discreet about their relationship, considering both the sensibilities of the Bible Belt town and her position in it, she knew from the sideways glances she'd noticed lately that it was being talked about. Apparently, Laurie Greene had taken it upon herself to speak to her about what had developed between them.

"I was just wondering, since things seem to have calmed down around here..." Laurie hesitated. "I mean, the investigation *is* over, isn't it?"

"Of the kidnapping?"

Laurie nodded.

"Our part of it at least," Eden agreed, at a loss now as to what this could possibly be about.

"I didn't want to ask while y'all were so busy, and it's silly, really. Link said to just let it go, but... The thing is,

Moxie—that's our dog, you know—likes her little quilt. I like it, too, 'cause it just fits in her bed, and besides that, it washes like a dream. And Dean promised me we could have it back when the evidence people were through with it. He said that might take weeks, but it's been that now. So if they are, through with it, I mean, can I get it back?"

"The quilt." Eden had repeated the words to give herself time to think, but the phrase Laurie had used was the only thing in her head. *Dean promised me we could have it back...*

"The pink gingham one. Link used it to cover the seat of the truck when he took Moxie to the vet that day. Then, because she'd got it dirty, he just threw it in the back. It's a wonder it didn't blow out while he was driving home."

"That was *your* quilt?"

Laurie's mouth opened, but apparently something in Eden's voice or expression made her think better of whatever she had been about to say. "It doesn't matter. You just send it back to me when you get through. Y'all grilling tonight?" She glanced down at the package Eden's fingers were resting on.

"We are," Eden managed to say.

"Well, you have fun. Major Underwood seems like a very nice young man."

Eden smiled, still trying to assimilate the information that had just fallen into her lap. "He is. He really is."

"You take care now, you hear." With that, Laurie Greene, who sat in the front row of the Pentecostal church every Sunday, put her stamp of approval on Jake and then put her shopping cart into motion.

Eden turned back to the cooler, using her supposed perusal of its contents as an excuse not to meet anyone's eyes while the events of the night they'd found that quilt played through her head like a movie. Her reaction to it. Dean's comment that she looked as if she'd seen a ghost. If he had somehow known about Christie's kidnapping, the rest would have been easy enough to put together.

Had her deputy chief carried out that campaign of terror? Was Dean, whom she not only considered a colleague, but also a friend, capable of that kind of duplicity? And if so, for what reason?

She realized the answer to that had occurred to her more than once during the course of the investigation into Raine's abduction. Dean believed he was better equipped to be Chief of Police of Waverly than she was.

She picked up the steaks she'd considered and wheeled her buggy to the front. As she stood in the checkout line, memories from those frantic days ran endlessly through her head.

Her first impulse was to find Jake. To tell him what she'd learned. He would know exactly what to say to put this into perspective. She couldn't think of anyone she knew whose advice on how to deal with this kind of betrayal she would value more than his.

Except maybe, she admitted, as she walked to her car, that of the man who had stood at her side for the past three years. A man who had been her mentor, her second-in-command and—or so she had thought—her friend.

IN THE END, she had opted to handle this on her own. Jake couldn't fight her battles for her. She didn't want him to.

She walked into the station and then back to Dean's office. Now, at the end of his workday, he was sitting with his feet up on the desk, hands behind his head.

As soon as he saw her, he straightened. "I thought you had gone for the day."

"I was. Then I ran into Laurie Greene at Publix." She could tell by the way his face changed that he knew what was coming.

It was all so stupid. Didn't he think about the possibility that one of the Greenes might say something to her about the quilt? Or was the opportunity to get back at her too good to pass up, so that he had decided he'd deal with the fallout, if there was any, when it came?

"Yeah? How's she doing?"

"She wants her quilt. It seems you promised she could have it back when the state lab was done."

Dean's lips pursed, but he didn't attempt to deny or explain. He just sat there, waiting.

"How did you know about my sister?"

"Your daddy was a real good law-enforcement officer. I ought to know. I worked with him for fifteen years." He shrugged. "Being a pretty good officer myself, I got curious about what he was doing on all those trips he took. Once I did, it didn't take much effort to find out what had happened."

"You never once mentioned her disappearance to me. Not even when Raine was taken."

"I wasn't sure how much of it you remembered. I didn't want to—"

"Bring up painful memories?" she finished when he stopped.

"For what it's worth, I'm sorry I did what I did."

He still hadn't put it into words, Eden realized. Maybe he wasn't capable of admitting how low he'd stooped. *Being a pretty good officer myself...*

"What I don't understand is why. What was the point, Dean?"

"You'd lost your objectivity. Buying into what Underwood was telling you. I thought maybe the other was affecting your judgment."

"The other? My sister's kidnapping? You thought that was interfering with my ability to do my duty, so you decided to re-create events related to it? Were you hoping I'd have a breakdown and just turn the job over to you?"

"I thought," he said evenly, "considering your situation, that I was better equipped to lead the investigation."

"You thought Raine was *dead*. How the hell could that *possibly* have made you 'better equipped' to find her?"

"The agents thought she was dead."

"And they were wrong, *too*. What I don't get is you doing something like that when everybody else is out searching for a missing child. Trying desperately to find her before she could be murdered."

"So was I," he said indignantly. "I worked as hard as anybody on that case. That's one thing you can't accuse me of. Slacking on my duty."

"But while you were doing your duty," she repeated sarcastically, "you had time to break into my house and pull pranks. How'd you get in, by the way?"

He hesitated, but he told her. After all, what difference could it make now?

"I made a copy of your door key. You always leave yours lying around."

Because of their bulk, she usually tossed her ring of keys on top of the bookcase beside her office door as she came in each morning.

"I want it." She held out her hand.

After a long moment he reached into his desk drawer and then laid the single key on her palm.

"And I want your badge."

The shock in his eyes was gratifying. She wasn't sure what he had thought she was going to do about what he'd done, but firing him clearly wasn't it.

"You're joking."

She laughed. "Unlike you, I wouldn't do something like that. Play with somebody's emotions."

"What I did wasn't a firing offense. You'll have a hard time explaining that to the town *and* to the rest of the department."

"You know, I don't think I will. I suspect that, like me

when they find out what you were up to while the rest of us were trying to find Raine, they'll applaud my getting rid of you. And if they don't, then I'll deal with any objections they have when they make them. As Chief of Police, that's my job."

"One you were never entitled to," he said bitterly.

It was almost a relief to have it out in the open. Something she had suspected from the first.

"I have a degree in criminal justice. The mayor and the city council believed that qualified me."

"Your daddy badgered them into hiring you."

"I don't doubt he had influence. But they had options. And they chose not to take them."

"They chose a piece of paper over years of experience."

"Apparently, experience doesn't necessarily come with integrity. Give me your badge."

She thought for a moment he was going to refuse. Instead he unpinned the emblem of authority he'd worn during his long service to the town and put it in her outstretched hand.

"You'll regret this."

She smiled again as her fingers closed around the badge, so tightly that the metal edges bit into her palm. "Thanks for the warning, but I don't think so."

He held her eyes, and then, seeing nothing in them but the determination she felt to get this over and done with, he picked up his hat and stalked to the door. "I'll come tomorrow to clean out my office."

"I'll have somebody do that for you. On behalf of Waverly, thank you for your service. And for what it's worth, you're right. You were a pretty good police officer. Until you forgot what that's all about."

Dean's lips tightened, but he didn't say anything else. And the sound of his angry footsteps retreating down the hallway was satisfying on a level Eden almost felt guilty about.

"How was your day?" Jake asked, as she put the groceries down on his kitchen table.

She looked up to find him in the kitchen doorway, hair still damp from his shower.

"Interesting." Reaching into one of the bags, she began to put away the things they wouldn't need for tonight. "I'll tell you about it over this." She held up the bottle of red wine she'd bought to go with the steaks. "What have you been up to?"

"Plowing the south forty?" he suggested with a grin.

"Since the south forty is mostly swamp, I don't think so."

Her smile invited him into the room. When he put his arms around her, the familiar scent of the soap he used surrounded her like the welcome warmth of a fire on a winter's night.

"You smell good," she murmured, her lips against his neck.

"You *feel* good." His hands slid down her spine to cup under her bottom.

"Yes, I do," she said, pushing away from him to complete the unpacking.

"Somebody's mighty pleased with herself."

"Yes, somebody is. And with you," she added with another smile.

"Good. Because I've been thinking."

When he didn't go on, she looked up from the potatoes she'd just placed on the counter beside the sink. Despite the way their relationship had progressed in the past few weeks, she felt a frisson of anxiety.

"About what?"

No promises. No guarantees. Those had been the rules when they'd begun this, and if he had decided now that what they were doing—

"That I'm going to hate like hell for you to go home tonight. And that I hate like hell when I have to leave your place."

"I told you—"

"I'm not suggesting we scandalize the town. Scandalizin

my grandmother is bad enough. I expect her ghost to start haunting me any day. Warning me to mend my wicked ways." The line of his mouth was tilted.

A good sign, Eden told herself. He wasn't going to walk away. Not like this. Not while making jokes about his grandmother.

"Considering your...shall we say...*colorful* past, if Miz Etta hasn't given you that message before now, I doubt she's going to."

"The thing is, I have a suspicion there *are* a couple of messages she'd like to give me."

"Like what?" She was smiling, too. Relaxed, now that she knew this wasn't going where she'd feared it might.

So much for not making promises. Definitely not all it was cracked up to be.

"Like...it would be nice if I could leave my truck in front of your house all night, and nobody would say anything about it."

She'd been reaching up to get the cheese grater down from the top shelf. She looked over her shoulder to smile at him. "Then Miz Etta wouldn't be the only one who'd be giving you messages."

Jake moved behind her to retrieve the grater. "I said if nobody had anything to say about it."

"They would. Believe me. And don't tell me we're in the twenty-first century. We're also in Waverly."

Only after she'd turned to face him did she realize how close he was. Close enough that she wasn't sure the steaks weren't going to have to wait.

"Not if..." He hesitated again, looking down into her eyes. He put his hands on the countertop on either side of her body. "I told you I'm no bargain, but..." He took a breath. "I think Miz Etta would be very pleased if I made an honest woman of you."

An honest woman. Twist the words how she might, there seemed to be only one meaning for that phrase. "As in…?"

"You, me. Some great-grandkids for her."

Despite the fact that he'd just asked her to marry him, Jake's eyes revealed his uncertainty. And she couldn't stand seeing it there.

"Yes," she said softly. "Oh, my goodness, yes. I really think Miz Etta deserves that."

"No reservations?"

"Not a one. I love you, Jake Underwood. I love everything about you. Even this." She put her fingers over the depression at his temple, but he turned his head slightly so they no longer touched the injury.

When he looked back at her, however, he was smiling. "I love you, too. More than I ever thought it would be possible for me to love a woman."

"I think Waverly—*and* Miz Etta—will definitely approve. After all, you *are* a hero."

"You just keep thinking that, sunshine."

"I will," she vowed softly, stretching upward for his lips. "For the rest of my life, I promise you."

* * * * *

Harlequin

INTRIGUE

COMING NEXT MONTH

Available September 13, 2011

#1299 THE BLACK SHEEP SHEIK
Cowboys Royale
Dana Marton

#1300 DETECTIVE DADDY
Situation: Christmas
Mallory Kane

#1301 SCENE OF THE CRIME: WIDOW CREEK
Carla Cassidy

#1302 PHANTOM OF THE FRENCH QUARTER
Shivers: Vieux Carré Captives
Colleen Thompson

#1303 THE BIG GUNS
Mystery Men
HelenKay Dimon

#1304 WESTIN'S WYOMING
Open Sky Ranch
Alice Sharpe

> You can find more information on upcoming
> Harlequin® titles, free excerpts and more at
> **www.HarlequinInsideRomance.com.**

HICNM0811

New York Times *and* USA TODAY *bestselling author*
Maya Banks presents a brand-new miniseries

PREGNANCY & PASSION

When four irresistible tycoons face
the consequences of temptation.

Book 1—ENTICED BY HIS FORGOTTEN LOVER

Available September 2011 from Harlequin® Desire®!

Rafael de Luca had been in bad situations before. A crowded ballroom could never make him sweat.

These people would never know that he had no memory of any of them.

He surveyed the party with grim tolerance, searching for the source of his unease.

At first his gaze flickered past her, but he yanked his attention back to a woman across the room. Her stare bored holes through him. Unflinching and steady, even when his eyes locked with hers.

Petite, even in heels, she had a creamy olive complexion. A wealth of inky-black curls cascaded over her shoulders and her eyes were equally dark.

She looked at him as if she'd already judged him and found him lacking. He'd never seen her before in his life. Or had he?

He cursed the gaping hole in his memory. He'd been diagnosed with selective amnesia after his accident four months ago. Which seemed like complete and utter bull. No one got amnesia except hysterical women in bad soap operas.

With a smile, he disengaged himself from the group

around him and made his way to the mystery woman.

She wasn't coy. She stared straight at him as he approached, her chin thrust upward in defiance.

"Excuse me, but have we met?" he asked in his smoothest voice.

His gaze moved over the generous swell of her breasts pushed up by the empire waist of her black cocktail dress.

When he glanced back up at her face, he saw fury in her eyes.

"Have we *met?*" Her voice was barely a whisper, but he felt each word like the crack of a whip.

Before he could process her response, she nailed him with a right hook. He stumbled back, holding his nose.

One of his guards stepped between Rafe and the woman, accidentally sending her to one knee. Her hand flew to the folds of her dress.

It was then, as she cupped her belly, that the realization hit him. She was pregnant.

Her eyes flashing, she turned and ran down the marble hallway.

Rafael ran after her. He burst from the hotel lobby, and saw two shoes sparkling in the moonlight, twinkling at him.

He blew out his breath in frustration and then shoved the pair of sparkly, ultrafeminine heels at his head of security.

"Find the woman who wore these shoes."

Will Rafael find his mystery woman?
Find out in Maya Banks's passionate new novel
ENTICED BY HIS FORGOTTEN LOVER
Available September 2011 from Harlequin® Desire®!

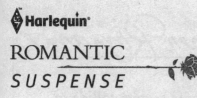

Harlequin®
ROMANTIC
SUSPENSE

NEW YORK TIMES BESTSELLING AUTHOR
RACHEL LEE

The Rescue Pilot

Time is running out…

Desperate to help her ailing sister, Rory is determined
to get Cait the necessary treatment to help her fight
a devastating disease. A cross-country trip turns into
a fight for survival in more ways than one when their plane
encounters trouble. Can Rory trust pilot Chase Dakota
with their lives, and possibly her heart?

**Look for this heart-stopping romance in September
from *New York Times* bestselling author Rachel Lee
and Harlequin Romantic Suspense!**

Available in September wherever books are sold!